OH YOU PRETTY THING

By the same author
The Comedienne
The Woman in Beige
Diary of a Provincial Lesbian
As You Step Outside
Always You, Edina
Mr Oliver's Object of Desire

OH YOU PRETTY THING
VG LEE

Tollington

First published in 2019 by Tollington Press, Machynlleth, Wales, UK
Reprinted 2022
www.tollingtonpress.co.uk

Copyright © VG Lee 2019
VG Lee asserts the moral right to be identified as the author of this work.
www.vg-lee.com

All rights reserved. No part of this book may be reproduced or transmitted, in any form or by any means, without permission.

A catalogue record for this book is available from the British Library.

ISBN 978-1-909347-13-7

Design by Helen Sandler
Printed and bound in the UK by Biddles Books Ltd

Versions of two of these stories appeared in *Men & Women*, ed. Paul Burston (Glasshouse, 2011) and the Kenric anthology *We want to tell you how…*, ed. Stephanie Dickinson and Pat Dungey (Paradise, 2018).

Contents

Foreword	7
Flint Road	9
Sweet	15
We Share a Party Wall	41
A Day Spent with Deirdre	59
The Time of Their Lives:	
I Friends & Family	67
II Father & Daughter	94
III The Lovely Nieces	105
IV The Three of Us	125
Lucky Patricia	139
For the Love of Estelle	153
Oh You Pretty Thing:	
Part 1	166
Part 2	185
Part 3	200
Alpaca Moonlight	215

Foreword

I was asked recently why so many of my short stories had unhappy endings, but in this collection I can promise that some will end happily. These stories were written over a period spanning the last twenty years. Some are entirely fictional, but many are based on or inspired by my own experiences and personal observations. Here are comedy, romance, friendship and family, love and loss.

Central to the book are three longer stories. 'Sweet' is a piece of historical fiction, set in Idaho at the beginning of the twentieth century. The title story, 'Oh You Pretty Thing', is a novella that incorporates elements of my own earlier life: a young, quite thoughtless married woman realises she has made the wrong life choice. Finally, 'The Time of Their Lives' is a narrative in four sections about growing up in a one-parent family. One of these stories touches on my own experience of childhood abuse, an area I've never addressed before through my writing.

With the exception of a couple of stories, I've written these primarily for lesbian readers. Not intentionally, but the themes reflect my own history, and I've spent a long time as part of the lesbian community.

This is my second collection of stories and a chance to put together work which has (mostly) not been seen before. I think there is a story here for everyone – or at least, I hope so.

VG Lee, Sussex, January 2019

FLINT ROAD

Marianne doesn't feel nervous in the empty house, even though it's detached, set back from the road, and at some distance from any neighbours. Upstairs in the two bedrooms it seems particularly stuffy and she opens the windows, anxious that when she comes to sell or let the house, black mould will have started to creep across the walls. Years ago, living here with Ruth, she would never have worried over such things.

The only stick of furniture left behind is the rocking chair that once belonged to her grandmother. Everything else in the house she and Ruth divided up, taking turns to choose. She remembers how even then, with Ruth leaving her for someone else, she still put Ruth's choices first, knowing the items she had a particular fondness for.

Marianne pulls the rocking chair nearer to the window and sits looking down over the sunlit garden. They always did let it grow wild, but now in late April it is truly a wilderness, all shades of lush green. Through Ruth, she came to appreciate birds and insects and... just nature. Together, late in the evening, they would watch every kind of small animal: badgers, foxes, hedgehogs, even a mole. Once Ruth was convinced she'd seen a lynx but it turned out to be a harmless black feral cat. They called him Percy.

But now something needs to be done out there, decisions made.

Marianne's relationship with Ruth lasted a very long time. Within a year of it finishing, she embarked on a new relationship, which went well at first. It was a relief to be part of a couple once more and she genuinely liked the woman. In time she assumed that this liking would grow into love. But do you know, she'd used up so much emotion and energy in the longer relationship, after a few months Marianne realised she had nothing of any value to give to someone else.

Intimacy was the chief stumbling block. She'd shared all her secrets once before. Really, *all* her secrets. During that long relationship she'd learnt to trust. They shared one another's past histories and on discovering each point of similarity their bond grew deeper, at least on Marianne's side. The similarities were good but when you're in love, differences can be even more interesting.

"I never enjoyed walking till I met you." Or music festivals, or red wine, or holidays in Scotland, voting Green… and of course they adopted Percy. Marianne had never owned any animal before and if asked would have said she preferred dogs or even spider monkeys. This last wasn't true but Marianne liked to make Ruth smile.

Percy missed Flint Road. He was never truly Marianne's cat; his affections always lay with Ruth. From that same back door, Marianne had often watched the two of them out in the garden: years and years of Percy hiding behind or in or under the holly bush and Ruth singing a little song to herself and strolling past the bush as if she had no idea that Percy was there. Percy leaping out, front paws in the air, before pelting up the garden and back to her.

"Clever boy." Ruth stroking the cat from the top of his head, along his back to his tail. Percy looking up at her with adoring green eyes.

Marianne had always imagined cats to be heartless creatures but Percy changed that opinion forever.

Sometimes Ruth tried to turn the tables on him by suddenly stopping in front of the holly bush and shouting "Boo!" Percy refused to be either surprised or alarmed. He'd step out from his hiding place and award Ruth a disapproving stare as if she'd committed an act of bad taste. Which made her laugh.

"Sorry Percy," she'd say.

Yes, Percy had loved Ruth, and the garden, and the house with its wide windowsills and dark corners on the stairs. And Ruth had loved Percy, yet she hadn't taken him with her. She'd said, "Marianne, I can't bear to leave you on your own."

When Marianne and her new lover decided to share a flat together, Marianne put Percy into a cattery, just for a month. She reasoned that time on his own in a different but safe environment would make the eventual change of home easier for him. There'd be a chance for memories to blur. She reasoned as if Percy was a child she'd parted from his mother, but if she assumed that the cat would forget Ruth or Flint Road, she was wrong.

Percy came back from the cattery a little bewildered but he didn't appear too traumatised. The flat, about a mile away from Flint Road, was small but with a pretty garden and several established shrubs for Percy to hide in. As directed by the cattery she kept Percy indoors for a month. In that time, he dramatically lost weight. It was as if he'd been holding on in the expectation that Ruth would eventually come for him, as if he couldn't believe in her desertion.

Percy is only a cat and yet even these memories remain so hard for Marianne to recall.

It was a relief when the month passed to finally let him out in the new garden. Marianne felt sure that once Percy went outside he'd start to thrive again but on the second morning there was no sign of him anywhere. They searched. They called. The new partner assured her that the cat would come back in a few hours. She offered all manner of consoling opinions on feline behaviour, although she'd never owned a cat herself.

He didn't come back. Marianne went through the streets calling his name and banging on a cat food tin with a spoon. The new partner wanted to join her but no; Percy would never show himself to this relative stranger.

Days later, as a last resort, on an old friend's advice, Marianne returned to Flint Road. She stood at the open kitchen door and called for him. It was a still morning just after seven. She saw the long grass at the end of the garden shiver and then the shiver began to head in her direction. Finally, Percy burst out into the open and raced towards her. Afterwards she told the new partner, "He looked so hopeful. His eyes such a bright green and grass seeds hanging from his whiskers."

When he realised it was only Marianne, he'd slowed, stepping towards her at a much more dignified pace. She closed the inner door and once he was in the room she quickly shut the back door. He fought her when she tried to lift him into the cat basket. He wriggled and scratched and growled furiously as if he saw her as an enemy.

A week later he disappeared again. Marianne came straight back to Flint Road but Percy wasn't so easy to catch. On four consecutive days she returned and finally from hunger he was tempted into the house. This time when she put him in the basket he didn't struggle, which upset her even more.

Sitting in the chair gently rocking herself, Marianne feels she resembles an elderly female character from a horror film or a Bette Davis movie, a woman still wounded by a tragic past. She should have hung on to one of their six straight-backed dining chairs. A less comfortable chair wouldn't have encouraged her to relax and begin dwelling on painful topics while she put off the moment of finally locking up the house.

Thinking about Ruth is still so upsetting. She has to make an effort every moment of every day to resist the need to cry. Her heart truly continues to feel broken but, with difficulty, she is making some sense of her life. She won't look for someone else. She's tried that and it didn't work. Nor was it fair to use another person to heal a wound. For seventeen years Marianne lived with Ruth and was happy on most days. Having a love that lasted so long is pretty good for a lifetime. Not everybody gets that much.

Back at the flat, the new love (who was never really a love at all) has gone. Marianne and Percy are happier. He goes out in the small garden now and doesn't try to escape, although Marianne thinks that if he heard Ruth's voice calling him, even at a distance, he'd be off without a backward glance. Marianne wouldn't blame him. If she heard Ruth's voice calling for *her*, she too would answer the call.

Wearily, Marianne gets to her feet. She closes the windows and goes downstairs, leaving the rocking chair moving slightly.

The sun has disappeared behind what Marianne still thinks of as 'Percy's holly bush'. She has been in the house for hours.

In the kitchen are the dregs of a mug of tea she made earlier. She brought biscuits with her but now it's time to leave. She washes out the mug and returns it to an empty cupboard. She allows herself one last look at the garden. None of her friends know that she still owns this house. If they did, they would tell her to 'get rid, cut ties, move on'.

About to turn away, she notices a shiver of movement running through the long grass at the end of the garden. She holds her breath, fearful of being disappointed. Percy emerges. He doesn't hurry. If a cat can appear thoughtful, that is how he appears. By the time Marianne has reached the open kitchen door, Percy is already there, his tail held up in greeting.

She steps aside and lets him enter. In passing he rubs his head against her knee.

"What are you doing here?" she says. "Your dinner's at home."

Ignoring Marianne, Percy leaps onto a windowsill. For a moment he looks at her before turning to stare out into the darkening garden. From the set of Percy's ears, the slightly raised fur on his back, she can tell he is aware of her every move. Is he waiting for the inevitable? For her to gather him up and return him to their shared half-life?

She reaches a decision that is so obvious, she could easily laugh or cry with relief. From the cupboard, she retrieves the mug and places it next to the kettle. She gathers up her carrier bag and jacket, debating whether to close and lock the kitchen door. She decides to leave it wide open. For now, there is nothing here to steal.

As if the cat is a child, she reassures him: "Wait for me, Percy. I'm coming back."

SWEET

Princess Diana is dancing with someone I vaguely recognise as the film star John Travolta. The princess and her husband Charles are at a Gala Dinner in Washington given by President Ronald Reagan and his wife Nancy. Diana looks lovely. She wears a midnight-blue velvet dress with a sparkly jewelled choker around her neck. It is the stuff of romance: lovely young woman marrying a prince and her life is transformed. I wonder if she and her prince will be happy. The newsreel changes to shots of a shopping mall in Virginia and somewhere else in Palm Beach, Florida, where the prince will play polo. I switch off the set and pick up my needlework. In my imagination I'm no longer an old woman. I am a child again, the year is 1906 and I'm sewing leather buttons on Clothilde Morris's coat.

You may never have heard of Sweet, a small town in Idaho. Nor might it be your idea of a town, nor even a village. Main Street, as I think back, is a wide dirt track that becomes a quagmire in winter or when it rains. The wooden buildings set off the ground on stilts seem to be only *just* standing, although to my childish eyes that is how buildings (and people) are meant to be – at strange angles, leaning into each other!

My sister Lillie and I are orphans. Our parents died from cholera when I was too small to retain much memory of them, but we were taken in by Bertha, our mother's one friend.

Bertha is German. That is all we know about her background. People do not mull over the past – it is a case of move on or slip under. Bertha is a seamstress, laundress and purveyor of fine, second-hand linens bought from folk heading East or West, or from those forced to stay where they are because their pot of money has run dry. She is in her fifties, which is considered old. Her legs are full of water and when it is hot or cold or wet, she can hardly walk. In her swollen hands and feet, she has rheumatism, so as much as she is a godsend to us, we are a godsend to her. She has taught us to sew and cut patterns; to take garments in and out; to steam marks from a fine piece of taffeta; to wash, press and make good as new from the old and tired. She has taught us to be useful.

Our town has a resident population ranging from around five hundred to as many as a thousand depending on the season. Not large but, due to the Thunder Mountain Gold Strike five years earlier which brought money and optimism to Sweet, it boasts three saloons, three hotels and even a newspaper. I am ten at the time of this story and my big sister, Lillie, thirteen. We share a tiny room at the back of the laundry, our bunk beds alongside Bertha's bentwood chair and precious Singer sewing machine. From early on I have shown an aptitude for fine sewing. Under Bertha's tuition I more than earn my keep, whereas Lillie is clumsy and inattentive, only good for plain sewing or working in the laundry.

We are fed well. Each day, apart from Sunday, Bertha allows us fifteen minutes at one o'clock to eat our bread and meat washed down with a tin mug of water. We sit together on the step in the open doorway and look out over the street. We never say much to each other but I assume that Lillie is as fascinated by the bustling town as I am. I love to study the men, women and children, the horses, mules, wagons and carts. I am absorbed in the noise: the mix of loud calling voices against the crunch of turning wooden wheels and horses' hooves. In the summer, my world is the colour of sand, in winter everything turns to shades of grey.

Men by far outnumber women, which means that women stand out – they cannot go unobserved. I know many of the townswomen's names, the names of the time: Eliza, Lucille, Ida, Kitty and Nellie. Women with husbands, women looking for a husband, the school teacher who insists that she lives with her sister, although no two ladies were ever less alike! And the slatternly cook at the Carlton Hotel, who frequently recounts how she was a beauty till the age of twenty-five, when her teeth fell out by the handful. There are 'the girls' who work the Carlton Saloon. They wear red painted smiles and hitch their skirts high when crossing the street so that men can admire their calves and ankles.

The day my sister says *she* wants to work at the saloon, Bertha slaps her face hard for the first time ever. She has Mr Carlton come across to the laundry, stands Lillie in front of him and asks what he thinks of the idea. Mr Carlton is a handsome man and one of Bertha's best clients. Somehow, the dust of our town never sticks to his fine clothes or his clean, leathery skin.

Now Lillie might be dirty and to my eyes plain, but her youth alone is enough to make her a good proposition to join Mr Carlton's stable of females. But no, he tells her firmly that nobody launders his shirts and cravats like she does and that pretty young women (he pinches her cheek) can be got for less than a dollar from the cities, whereas a good laundress is worth her weight in gold. And of course, he is right.

Much later in the day, after Bertha has gone up to her room above the laundry, my sister sits hunched, staring at her hands. The knuckles and joints of her fingers are already beginning to swell like Bertha's and the skin is as rough as sandpaper from all the daily washing and steaming of other people's clothes and bedding. Her nails have been broken and discoloured for a long, long time.

Under her breath my sister mutters something.

"What's that you're saying?" I ask.

Louder she says, "Give me a year at the Carlton Saloon and these hands would be as clean and soft as any lady's hands."

While Lillie is womanly at thirteen, I am small for my age and thin and, I suppose, a child still. I don't look any further ahead than the next morning. I have no personal vanity and that perhaps will hold true throughout my life. I wear my hair permanently plaited. It seems to be a dark and dirty colour, although the few times Bertha has washed it, I have been surprised to discover a shade of silvery-gold. Bertha, when she saw how soft and shiny my hair was, said it was best if we never washed it again till I reached my sixties, lest I catch the eye of men like Mr Carlton! I am a quiet girl but interested in every darn thing. Bertha often tells me by way of a warning that curiosity killed the cat; but it never killed me.

It is the start of summer, a mid-afternoon. The temperature is high, our town a dustbowl. Wherever I walk the red and orange dust flies up and settles. Lillie and I are crossing Main Street, each clutching the handle of a covered basket full of freshly washed and ironed laundry. Mr Carlton, smart as ever in a brocade waistcoat, smokes a cigar on the balcony of one of the upper rooms of his saloon. His elbows resting on the rail, he surveys his kingdom. This section of Main Street as good as belongs to him. He exudes money and good living. As far as I'm concerned Mr Carlton is 'the treat of Sweet'. We look up at him and he acknowledges us with an expansive wave of his cigar.

And then comes the rumble of carriage wheels and thundering hooves: the very air is charged with excitement as the daily coach from Emmett, the nearest town and eleven miles away, rolls in. Quick as a flash Lillie and I whisk ourselves and our basket onto the sidewalk to watch. The street is suddenly packed as people stream out of the few shops, emerge from alleyways, peer from windows and doorways. Word has gone around, we know not from where it started; an arrival is expected, not a dull clerk or duller prospector, a 'youngish woman of some note'. These are the words I've heard repeated constantly over the last few days by Bertha's predominantly female customers.

The coach pulled by two pairs of horses comes to an untidy halt, the front horse trying to buck its way out of the traces. We see only one passenger inside the carriage but they make no attempt to get out. The driver alights. He tosses the reins down to a stable lad waiting in the road before dusting off his jacket and trousers, leaving his hat till last, then opening the coach door and letting the hinged set of wooden steps drop down. A moment passes and another. We wait, our gazes hungry. Finally, a small, velvet hat appears, of orange colour with a glossy black feather in the band. Ignoring the driver's proffered hand, a slender woman daintily takes the steps. She straightens up and eyes us all. And don't we all stare back at her? I imagine I read amusement in her face.

I judge the woman to be in her late twenties, early thirties, but I am most interested and impressed by her fine clothes: a duster coat of burnt orange the exact shade of her hat, fastened with two rows of jet buttons, worn over a newly fashionable hobble skirt, also edged in orange satin braid. And gloves and velvet purse, shoes of polished tan leather.

Lillie says, "She's very tall, taller than most men."

"She's lovely."

Lillie snorts. "Anyone would look lovely wearing clothes like that."

I'm half-inclined to agree with my sister.

On the other side of the street, Bertha stands in the shadow of the laundry. I wonder if she's been there all along, as curious as everyone else to see the new arrival.

"Get moving," she mouths at us.

We pick up the basket and head for the hotel, neither of us concentrating on where we are going because we're watching the woman's luggage, taken piece by expensive piece from the roof of the coach. So much of it. How long does she intend to stay?

There is not a woman in the town to compare with Clothilde Morris. Yes, she is tall. Her figure is full and shapely, her eyes are green, her hair is auburn shot with gold.

A few days following her arrival, Mr Carlton makes the remark to Bertha that "This new visitor reminds me of a fox – in colouring, but also there is something about her." He is lost for words. He shakes his head almost as if bewildered, then says, "A beautiful fox, of course."

Bertha, usually so sharp-witted, seems confused. "Her clothes are certainly beautiful," is all she answers.

Having settled into the best room in Mr Carlton's hotel, Clothilde Morris – twirling a silk parasol above her head – walks across to the laundry. Bertha is already in the doorway to meet her.

"I believe you have a child who sews well. I'd like to hire

her." Clothilde's voice is slightly nasal – not altogether a pleasant sound, but unforgettable. "I'm willing to pay good money."

"May has work to do here," Bertha says. But then the two of them step back out onto the sidewalk and Lillie and I hear nothing more.

"Why you and not me?" Lillie wants to know.

I shrug.

From that day onwards, I go to the hotel each afternoon to collect and deliver washing, sponge down skirts and jackets, sew on buttons and mend seams or hems. There is something about my small, sharp face and small, sharp, bony body that puts Clothilde Morris at ease with me. I am still childlike, boy-like rather than girl.

Often, she is out riding or visiting. She seems to know the two good families who own ranches nearby, and certain ladies from the church and the town Ladies Circle visit to take tea. Clothilde's room has a vast bay window looking out over Main Street, and sometimes when I'm sitting with Lillie on the laundry step eating our lunch, we can hear laughter and the clink of china.

New drapes and swags are ordered from Bertha, also bed linen. I am set to unpack Clothilde's luggage and the packages that arrive for her several times a week containing mirrors, lamps of coloured glass, a silver hairbrush set, jewel-coloured rugs which she scatters across the newly polished floorboards. The bleak hotel room is transformed.

Twice a week flowers are sent in. Clothilde arranges these herself in blue and white vases – Jasperware vases, she tells me, imported and priceless. On one occasion a bouquet of lilac arrives and that is the first time I see Clothilde angry. She roughly grabs up the fragile pale mauve blossoms as if they possess no beauty at all, carries them out to the landing and drops them over the bannisters. She shouts after them, "Lilac are bad luck – not that I'd expect any of you ignoramuses to know that!"

There are afternoons when Clothilde's bad moods overwhelm her. She lies on her bed and broods while I quietly go about my work. Next to her bed is a gilt-framed photograph of a boy about six years old and she takes that up and holds it to her breast. I never ask who the boy is; I wait for her to tell me and finally she does.

"He is my son," she says.

I answer nothing, but nothing is what she expects of me. I lower my head over my needlework.

After a moment has passed she adds, "He lives with my husband." There is hatred in the way she says the word 'husband'.

I am sewing new buttons on her orange coat. The black jet buttons have been replaced by ones covered in leather and it is hard to get my needle through the stiffened eyelets.

"Did you hear what I said, May?"

"Yes." My voice is a whisper. I peer at her from under my eyelashes.

"I am on probation. Do you know what that means?"

I shake my head.

"I've been banished to this benighted town to see how long I can maintain a state of good behaviour." Clothilde rolls over on the bed so that her back is towards me. "You can go now, May."

Months pass. As I mend a tear in a dress or hem a set of Mr Carlton's handkerchiefs, I hear others wondering over why such a woman would choose to live in a hotel in a small town in the middle of nowhere. I contribute nothing to the puzzle. Answers are concocted that have long noses and fast running feet. Clothilde Morris is waiting for money to arrive and then she'll buy a ranch on the edge of town, or she intends to build a grand house with pillars and a ballroom; she is in hiding from a cruel (but rich) husband, or she waits for a rich (but ailing) husband to arrive. All the gossip surrounding her remains full of goodwill. We have never experienced a woman like Clothilde in our town before. It is like having a famous actress in our midst. Maybe, someone suggests, she *is* a famous actress? She gives the town a certain *cachet*. Clothilde is endlessly interesting. Everything she does, says, wears or buys is reported on the Sweet human telegraph.

It is the end of June, coming up to the Independence Day celebrations, when our self-styled mayor, George Cotton, announces there will be a 'Grand Dance' held in the reception room of the recently built Town Hall. Within hours, Bertha is swamped with orders for alterations, laundering and, for her wealthier clients – numbering a mere handful – new dresses, shirts and waistcoats are commissioned. My leisurely visits to the hotel cease abruptly. Lillie is sent as my replacement to pick up and deliver Clothilde's laundry while I'm set to work eighteen hours a day with needle and thread. Inexorably, Bertha sits at her sewing machine, swollen feet pumping the treadle. I am exhausted but happy and as excited as if I'm one of the guests. Bertha is content because the money she is making will see us well into the next year. Only Lillie is angry and resentful. She will not be at the dance and all these new clothes have nothing at all to do with her.

The day before the dance, Clothilde sails into the laundry,

bypassing Lillie blue-bagging and hand-finishing Mr Carlton's ruffled dress shirt, past me, perched on a stool in front of the window where there is the most light to see my sewing. She stops in front of Bertha, who is intent on pinning a paper pattern to a length of taffeta.

"Bertha!"

Bertha's mouth is full of pins but she looks up.

"I want May to act as maid for myself and my friend, tomorrow."

Bertha wipes the pins from her mouth. In her impassive German accent, she says, "Can't be done."

"Of course it can. You know I'll pay well."

"I have never been so busy. May's needed here."

"Any sewing work May has to do will surely be finished by four pm." Clothilde taps one foot on the stone floor. "I'll expect her at the hotel no later than four thirty."

Bertha is almost smiling. "Two dollars."

Clothilde steps backwards but I know she's only pretending to be shocked. "You drive a hard bargain."

"And fifty cents for her sister's disappointment."

It is Clothilde's turn to attempt a smile. She looks me over, from filthy hair right down to my equally grubby bare feet. "Can you tidy May up?"

"This isn't New York City," Bertha says.

The next day Bertha finds time to wash me in the same soap suds and water already used for several loads of laundry. This is my first ever bath. The sensation of being immersed into tepid grey water thick with scum is not pleasant. I struggle but my sister holds my arms above my head so that I can't even kick out with my legs.

"If you continue to fight us, we will drown you," Bertha

says, her voice cold and unfriendly. I believe her. I let them flay me with a scrubbing brush. As my white skin appears in patches from beneath the dirt I'm fascinated. It is as if I am newly minted. They manhandle me out of the wash tub and I stand on the cold stone floor while Lillie dries me with a remnant of cloth. Bertha climbs upstairs to her room and comes back with a faded and patched dress in grey wool. It has a whiteish collar and cuffs. She also brings a petticoat and a pair of drawers. Neither of these items have I ever needed to wear before. Once dressed, they drag a wooden comb through my tangled hair, bundle my waves into a bunch at the nape of my neck and tie it tightly with a piece of velvet ribbon. Bertha produces a pair of black boots. I have never worn boots or shoes before. These pinch my toes and heels.

"They're leather," she says as if that more than makes up for the tight fit.

Carrying my needlework bag, I hobble out of the laundry. From the other side of the road I glance back. Bertha is sitting on the front step smoking her clay pipe. She wears the pleased expression of a job well done. Our eyes meet and she almost smiles.

On the stroke of four thirty by the grandfather clock in the hotel lobby, I clump up the stairs to Clothilde's room. I hear laughter and an unfamiliar voice. I knock and the door swings open.

"Oh, my goodness." The unfamiliar voice is deep and almost masculine. Both Clothilde and the woman with her are in their underclothes.

With my head down, I clump into the room.

"What have we here?" The stranger tries to lift my chin but I resist. "A hobgoblin, is it?"

"Don't tease her, Eva. May, take off those ridiculous boots."

I sit on the floor but am completely flummoxed by the knotted laces. Eventually Clothilde kneels down and undoes them for me. Already a red weal has formed across my toes.

"I thought *she* was supposed to be the maid, not the other way around," Eva grumbles good naturedly.

A small suitcase lies open on the bed. Clothilde explains, "Tonight, Eva will wear these clothes, but they have been crushed on the journey."

I am set the task of taking out each garment and pressing it with the flat iron warming on the hearth. As I arrange the clothes in the order I will attend to them, I study this Eva woman. She wears a dusky brown dress of good quality. Her hair also is brown, parted in the middle and worn in a knot at the nape of her neck. Her face is pleasing but plain. She wears no jewellery.

From the suitcase I remove a grey three-piece suit, a waistcoat in embroidered satin, a linen shirt and even men's underclothes. These last, I am familiar with from working in a laundry. This friend Eva is a woman who intends, in a public place, to dress as a man.

It is rare but not impossible to see a woman wearing buckskins or just worn-out male attire when obliged to do a man's job. When I was a little girl, the infamous Pearl Hart dressed as a man to hold up a stage coach. She served only a short sentence in an Arizona prison. But to wear such clothes to a dance? A grand dance inaugurating the new Town Hall?

I have been nowhere, know nothing about the world outside this small Idaho town, yet I've been exposed to much. Invisible as an orphan working at a lowly job may be, I've observed the social customs, the way a decent woman is expected to behave. As yet these customs don't affect me, but they will affect a woman like Clothilde, a woman who up till now has been highly respected and admired.

"What's going on in that little head of yours?" Clothilde asks me gently.

I look up from my work into her green eyes.

"Tell me."

"Does she ever speak?" Eva asks.

"Shush. May is timid." She frowns at Eva. "Which is why she suits me."

My voice almost a whisper, I say, "No one will like this."

They both know exactly what I mean.

"They're not supposed to." Clothilde grins down at me, showing a sharp little eye tooth I've never noticed before. "How often has this miserable little town held a dance? Once in a blue moon! A dance should be exciting, should leave us talking for days after, even years."

I know exactly what *she* means.

The two of them are ready. They are giggling and girlish. I have never seen Clothilde act this way before. It makes me uneasy. I am embarrassed for her and yet when I catch a glimpse of the reflected Clothilde as she sashays past the cheval mirror, I am dazzled by such rich colour, such beauty. Her low-cut gown is deepest red. She has rouge on her cheeks, her lips are painted scarlet and her eyes sparkle.

Eva apes a dandy. Had she a moustache to twirl, she would twirl it! She flaunts a Malacca cane. Its handle, shaped like a duck's head, is made of ivory. The cane is a present from Clothilde, and Eva is so pleased with the gift. Hand in hand, they stand at the open window that looks out over Main Street and kiss like lovers. I am shocked and anxious for them both as if I have become the adult here.

*

It is the morning after the dance, the hour before daybreak, and we lie in our bunk beds, Lillie above me. She witnessed the entire evening from the upper gallery of the Town Hall where she was called out to stitch a tear in a gown and sew a button on and pin a corsage... she even drank a cup of wine brought to her by Mr Carlton.

"They were over an hour late," she whispers. "The atmosphere in the hall was strange: a few couples dancing but everyone had their eyes on the doorway as if waiting for something to happen. Then suddenly I heard a woman's voice cutting through the music: *'Get your dirty hands off me.'* I looked down into the hall below and saw your friend Clothilde forcing her way onto the dance floor pulling a young fellow along with her. The dancing couples were darting to right and left to allow them through. It was like the parting of the Red Sea. Mr Carlton told me off for laughing but I found it funny seeing all the guests in disarray."

"And then what happened?"

"It seemed like at the same moment we all realised that this friend was a woman not a man. Everyone was shocked but nobody knew what approach to take. The music ended. The friend tucked Clothilde's hand under her arm and they went to the refreshment room."

Lillie throws her legs over the side of the bunk and slithers down to mine. "Move over," she says. "There's more."

She climbs in next to me and we lie turned towards each other, our faces only inches apart.

"After an age, they came back, hand in hand and laughing and smiling at each other. They may have been inebriated but I think it was all show, to make themselves the centre of attention."

I feel a sinking in the pit of my stomach. Lillie's words are painting a vivid picture. Clothilde Morris has thrown down a gauntlet and nothing will remain the same.

"The musicians faltered and looked up at Mr Carlton for instruction. He was still with me on the balcony." Her voice is full of pride at Mr Carlton's attention. "Clothilde called out, 'A waltz, if you please!' and the orchestra began to play. Nobody joined them on the dance floor. Clothilde's 'friend' took her in her arms and they began to waltz as if it was all perfectly normal. They danced well. I'll allow them that."

"How did they look together? Did it seem very odd?" My heart is breaking. I am jealous of the Eva woman but fearful of the consequences the evening will have.

At first Lillie is silent. Lillie can be nasty about almost anyone but I believe she is thinking hard and aiming for honesty. I am right – her words are thoughtful. At one point there is a catch in her voice. "May, I wanted to hate them both for being so careless of everyone's feelings but they looked... splendid. The woman dressed as a man was so much more gentlemanly and elegant than any other man in the room. Even Mr Carlton." Lillie pauses before finishing. "I've never seen that look on someone's face before and probably never will."

"What look? Who was looking at who?"

"The friend. The dandy. A passionate look as if she was capable of risking anything for her love."

"And Clothilde?" I have to ask. "How did she seem?"

Lillie's voice turns sharp. "Oh, of course she looked beautiful and danced well, but I believe her to be cold and uncaring."

This warms my heart. I want Clothilde to be cold and uncaring towards Eva. "What happened next?"

Lillie breathes in. "The waltz ended. Nobody clapped.

Clothilde and her friend embraced. They kissed each other on the lips."

"In front of everyone?" I am horrified. Not about them kissing – they had kissed in Clothilde's room – but at the repercussions.

"Mr Carlton, carrying his cigar, walked up to them. Your Clothilde turned towards him and said, 'Mr Carlton, which one of us would you like to partner for the next dance?' He answered," Lillie's voice at my ear is almost inaudible, "'I'd rather dance with a syphilitic cow than one of you two deviants.'"

Mr Carlton's response appals me. We have lived only fifty yards away from his hotel and saloon for ten years, he has brought us candy, rag dolls, sometimes even remembered our birthdays – I feel as if he has always looked on me and my sister with a fond and kindly eye. I've rarely heard him use harsh language to a woman. Mr Carlton raises his hat to women, his voice is low and respectful... I almost don't believe Lillie and yet I do believe her.

"He misunderstood," I tell her. "It was a bit of fun."

Lillie shakes her head. "Not to him, it wasn't."

For the next two days, Clothilde and her friend remain in their hotel room. I see no sign of them, not at the window, nor in the street. They have no visitors. Rumours run wild and Bertha's laundry is a place for women to congregate. Even those who didn't attend the dance have as strong an opinion as those who did. Lillie and I, we keep our heads and bodies bent over our work but we listen eagerly. We hear that Mr Carlton has asked them to leave his hotel, that a petition has been raised to force them to quit the town, that nobody is to speak to them or serve them food or drink. If they won't go of their own accord, then he will starve them out. The school teacher, who only a week ago here in the laundry declared, "To quote the suffragist, Elizabeth Cady Stanton, *the best protection any woman can have is courage* – and Clothilde Morris has courage by the bucket-load," now disavows her. Nowhere do I hear a dissenting voice. I see that men feel threatened and like fools; women are bewildered and uneasy. Everyone appears to believe they have been duped by Clothilde, and they are angry.

I am aware of Bertha's scrutiny. I trust Bertha. She has worked me hard but I believe she loves me. So often she has demonstrated this love: a light touch to my head or shoulder, a softening of her voice or glance. I know Lillie's opinion of Clothilde. Lillie has taken sides with the town, but what is Bertha thinking?

In the relative cool of the morning, Mr Carlton strolls in. Like the moon emerging from behind clouds, Lillie begins to shine, her head droops in swan-like fashion over the tub of washing and she sends him quick looks like silver darts. He ignores us both and heads for the back room where Bertha is seated at her sewing machine.

"A word," he says.

Bertha sets aside the blouse she is working on and struggles to get to her feet.

"Don't get up," Mr Carlton commands. "I know how it is, with creaky old bones." His voice is full of affection.

"Mr Carlton, what can I do for you?"

He looks for a door to close for some privacy but there is no door. He says, "You'll have heard about the rumpus at the dance the other evening?"

She nods but remains silent. Bertha's taciturnity is one of

her virtues, the reason she is trusted by so many people, but in this instance I can tell that Mr Carlton would welcome some remark to encourage him. He touches a spool of thread, unwinds a yard of rick-rack braid, studies Bertha's dressmaking shears as if he has never seen such a thing, before gruffly saying, "If you have any items belonging to the lady or ladies in question, I advise you to return them today. If they owe you money, see that you get it."

Bertha folds her swollen hands into her lap. This time she inclines her head rather than nods, as if Mr Carlton is proffering a thought very similar to her own.

"I'll send Lillie over in the next half-hour," she says.

Mr Carlton looks horrified. "Not Lillie. You'd be putting a young girl with her looks in grave moral danger. Send May. She doesn't know B from a bull's foot about anything!"

"Of course." This time Bertha does get to her feet. "Nobody's going to get hurt, are they?"

"Not if they do as I say." His voice is iron hard.

With a sigh, Bertha wraps up a skirt and jacket, the tacking stitches still in the hem and lapels. "Lillie, May, there is underwear outside on the washing line," she says. "Not dry yet but fold it carefully and bring it all in."

By the time we return Bertha has started filling the big cane basket with Clothilde's things. She lays a strip of tarpaulin over these to protect them from the damp underwear and a final strip to hide such personal items from prying eyes. She carries the basket to the doorway and sets it down.

"Can you manage this, May?" she asks. Her eyes lock with mine as I lift the basket.

It is incredibly heavy, yet I pick it up as if it weighs nothing. "Of course," I tell her.

Sweet

Main Street is quiet. There are people, but their heads are bowed and they keep their voices low. I am aware of being watched as I mount the sidewalk on the hotel side of the road. At his lookout point from the first-floor balcony of the saloon Mr Carlton taps his cigar in my direction but his expression is cold. A rustle of skirts passes me by and a woman hisses, "Deliver your washing and get out quick."

The hotel lobby is in shadow and feels welcomingly cool. Away from observation, I catch my breath before attempting the stairs. Above me, the door to Clothilde's room opens. I see her laughing face and, although I'm full of anxiety for her, I can't stop my own face from answering with a smile. I had expected tears, sombre expression, the hush of a funeral parlour, but no. Clothilde calls back over her shoulder, "Eva, help the child."

Eva wears corduroy trousers with suspenders, a soft plaid men's shirt, glossy men's leather shoes. How I envy her the freedom of those clothes. Even in my ragged dress it is difficult to run as I would like, to feel free. Lightly, she hurries down to meet me, grabs the basket handles and carries it to the top, taking the stairs two at a time.

"Hell's bells," she says. "What have we here – gold bars?"

I hesitate. Should I go?

"Hurry up, May, and get in here, before some do-gooder spirits you away."

I hurry. Inside the room all is chaos: suitcases, boxes and Clothilde's trunk lie open, clothes are strewn everywhere.

Eva closes the door and pulls me forward, then they both turn their attention to the basket, tossing the washing and mending this way and that.

"Bless Bertha," Clothilde says as she lifts out a canvas bag.

"I'm starving," Eva says. "Hurry up."

"Plates!"

"Clothilde, this is no time for plates!" Eva shouts. But already I am putting plates and cutlery on the table.

Bertha has sent good bread, pickle, ham, a wedge of cheese, even two shiny red apples – food I have rarely seen at home. From a cupboard Clothilde fetches a jug of red wine. She grins at me. "Bertha isn't our only friend. The school teacher."

They have eyes only for each other and their food. Sated a little, Eva breaks the cheese into crumbly pieces and pops them into Clothilde's open mouth like a mother bird feeding a chick. Then they remember me.

"May, get on with the packing." Clothilde glances at the mantel clock. "We leave mid-afternoon when this dreary little town is taking a siesta. Wrap my vases in the washing. I'm only carrying clothes. Let Carlton and his pals pick over everything else."

As I work, I listen to their chatter. How will they get away? The Emmett coach isn't due till the morning. Time passes and I'm growing nervous. Mr Carlton will be wondering why I've remained so long here. I want to leave but I can't bear to. I have a thought, a hope, a dream, but the correct words stick in my throat.

Finally, Clothilde turns to me. "Nearly done." She sits on the bed and watches me fold the last shawl. "May, I shall miss you."

Here is my chance and I take it. I say, "Will you have your little boy to comfort you?"

Clothilde's eyes are devoid of emotion. "I doubt that." She picks up the framed picture of her son and studies it. "But there may be other little boys in the future. Who knows?"

Hesitantly I ask, "Wouldn't you like a little girl instead?"

"Oh, my lord," Eva laughs. "Your semi-mute wants to go with us."

Sweet

Head to one side, Clothilde considers me.

My heart lifts. "I could be your servant. I can sew and mend as well as Bertha."

She seems almost thoughtful but then she sighs and tosses the picture into the suitcase. "You see, May, you're neither a little boy nor a little girl, you're a young woman." She takes Eva's hand. "I already have a *youngish* woman."

They are so in love, they need no one else. I see that. I get to my feet and pick up the empty basket. As I open the door I hope for one last word. Without turning her head towards me, Clothilde says softly, "Thank Bertha for her help."

I am heartbroken.

I stand at the top of the staircase, my back to Clothilde's closed door. I hear their hurried movements, their laughter and voices more subdued. They are preparing to leave in earnest now. Below me, in the hotel lobby, the afternoon sun streams through the windows, cruelly picking out the fake grandeur of patched and grubby velvet upholstery, the marks of wet glasses on the many occasional tables. I hear a man's footsteps and slowly begin my descent. Mr Carlton is waiting for me. He takes me firmly by the shoulder and steers me out onto the sidewalk.

His voice low and angry, he says, "What is going on up there? You've been two hours."

I wrench my arm from his grasp. I attempt to emulate Clothilde or even Eva – a clever young woman's voice. "Obviously," I say coolly, "Miss Morris and her friend are preparing to leave."

"But how? When?"

"Does it matter? I thought everyone *wanted* them to leave."

"Not before they've been taught a damn good lesson." His face is contorted. He has no control over his features. Never again will I think of Mr Carlton as 'the treat of Sweet'.

This is my chance for revenge on Clothilde and the spiteful Eva. I am not a semi-mute. I have words and I will say them!

From across the road a familiar voice calls out, "Mr Carlton, sir."

He looks up and frowns. "Not now, Lillie. Get back to your soapsuds."

Ignoring this, Lillie skips across the road towards us but she does not look quite like my sister. Her face is a clean oval and she has pinched her cheeks to give them colour. Her dirty bare feet look incongruous peeping out from beneath the folds of one of Clothilde's simple day-dresses. I see the untidy stitching at the uneven hem where Lillie has attempted to shorten the skirt.

His face registers surprise at her altered appearance, then he shrugs and turns back to me, his voice gentler. "Tell me what you know, May."

My young brain works fast. If this was just about Eva, I would consign her to her fate, but in my mind's eye I see Clothilde dragged from the hotel by Mr Carlton's men, hair streaming wildly over her bare shoulders. I cannot let this happen.

Behind Mr Carlton's softened expression, I know he is capable of any violent act.

Convincingly I lie, "A cart is coming for them at midnight once the town is sleeping."

"May, are you sure?"

"Quite sure." I am the only one to hear Clothilde's window quietly close above me. I hope I have given them time to make their getaway.

My sister lays her grubby hand on his immaculate jacket sleeve and for a moment he is distracted. "Mr Carlton," she says, "May is lying. She would do anything to protect that woman. They leave this afternoon at half past three."

He looks from one to the other of us, undecided who to believe. His gaze returns to Lillie. "How would you know, my little washerwoman?"

She smiles up at him. "I overheard Bertha arranging everything. They will be hidden in the laundry cart."

"That's a lie," I say.

Mr Carlton ignores me; all his attention is now fixed on Lillie. "And why would Bertha do that?"

Triumphantly Lillie says, "She is one of them."

He understands immediately. Ignoring me, Mr Carlton touches her cheek, drawing his index finger down her face and along her jawline. "Clever girl," he says.

Returned to the laundry that has been my home, I find that Bertha has gone. The bolts of cloth, the spools of thread, her needlework box, pins, braid, the rail of paper patterns, the tools of her trade, all have disappeared. The shelves and cupboards are empty, the bleak rooms wiped clean of all trace of her. Apart from the sewing machine and bentwood chair, she has bequeathed to us the two tin baths for washing clothes, a basket of wooden pegs and very little else. Bewildered, I turn to Lillie.

She shrugs, anger in her eyes. "Bertha risked our lives as well as hers, to help your friends." In her stolen dress, she looked taller, more womanly. "I gave her ample warning."

I am rendered speechless for a moment.

Her voice kinder, she says, "May, I want a better life than this. Mr Carlton will reward me."

"Surely, Bertha must have said something, left some message for me."

Lillie takes my hand and leads me to the bentwood chair. "Sit," she says. "The chair is yours, the sewing machine is yours. Don't worry about Bertha, she took a vast amount of money with her. Worry about yourself."

"Will the laundry cart come for them at half past three?"

My sister is already heading towards the door. "I very much doubt it – and even if it does…"

For two hours I sit on a stool in the doorway of the laundry, looking out over a deserted Main Street. Not once do I see either Clothilde or Eva at their window. One of Mr Carlton's men patrols the sidewalk, keeping an eye on the hotel, keeping an eye on me. Lillie has packed her few things and gone across the road. As Mr Carlton welcomed her in, he looked over at me and nodded in friendly fashion, as of old.

No laundry cart arrives. It is now a quarter to four and Eva has appeared at the window for the first time. She looks down at me. I keep my expression impassive. I cannot save them but Lillie is right, I must save myself. In my head I think how foolish this all is: a woman aping a man, two women kissing. Without Mr Carlton's fury, maybe the fuss would have died down. I wonder at his fury. I recall his embarrassment months ago while talking to Bertha about Clothilde resembling a fox. Did he have expectations? I push Mr Carlton out of my mind and think of the two women. Are they fools or are they brave? I'm inclined to think they are fools, that they could have chosen to live the lives they wanted but in secret.

Suddenly the hotel doors fly open and men spill out. The noise of their shouting fills the air. They seem many but I count only half a dozen – all familiar, all belonging to the saloon. I see Clothilde Morris, her auburn hair pulled loose about her shoulders. In every other respect she is dressed for travelling. For a moment I have hope, but then I see that a man holds each of her arms. They march her out into the middle of the road and then they throw her down into the dust, where she lies very still. Behind her comes Eva; her hands are tied, her shirt torn open, revealing her breasts. This is not the dandy I met in the hotel room, nor the gentlemanly, elegant fellow described by my sister – this is a terrified woman.

I cannot bear it. My stool topples over as I step forward. "Leave them alone, you bullies," I cry out. My voice is weak but even so it stills the men. They look at each other. I detect a hint of shame in their faces.

A gunshot splits the sky. The men look upwards to the balcony of the saloon where Mr Carlton stands, his handgun pointed directly at me. "Get inside, May," he shouts.

I shake my head. A bullet hits the dust two feet in front of me.

In the road, Clothilde raises herself on her arms, her mouth bleeding. "Child, do as he says."

I go inside. I push the rickety door shut. In the back room I sit at Bertha's sewing machine. In her hurry to leave, there is the sleeve of a blouse halted in the middle of a seam. I take this as a sign, a message to me. My feet on the treadle, I begin to sew.

I hear from the school teacher that, under Mr Carlton's supervision, the men used hot tar on Clothilde Morris's face and upper body before feathering her. I see her only once more, on the day her husband arrives in his own private coach to take her away. The skin of her face is red raw – from the tarring and the scrubbing required to remove it – but her eyes are still fierce. She looks at me just the once as she is bundled into the coach, inclines her head.

I think they killed Eva. Afterwards, Mr Carlton boasts, "If she behaves like a man, let her be treated like a man."

In the night I often wake, my pillow wet, and believe myself back in Sweet during that awful day. I switch on the bedside lamp and count familiar objects – the silk dressing gown hanging from the hook on the door, my magazine dropped to the floor as I succumbed to sleep – and I feel relief. But on other nights I wake from a different dream. I'm sitting in a hotel room, sewing leather buttons on a woman's coat. Clothilde is smiling down at me and I feel so perfectly content.

WE SHARE A PARTY WALL

Friday

DEREK

Lizzie will be away overnight, arriving home tomorrow evening. She's going to a friend's birthday party in Solihull. It's foolish but I feel rejected because, although I am still keeper of her house keys, she no longer asks me to feed her two cats.

"I'll give them extra," she insists. "They'll be fine for twenty-four hours."

Lizzie moved into the house next door just over two years ago. Apparently, she chose this Kings Heath part of Birmingham because she has friends living in the area. Right from the start I liked her. She's in her late forties. I've told her I'm in my early sixties, but I'm actually seventy-one. I believe I do look younger than my actual age, although now and then the arthritis in my left knee gives me away. I've kept myself fit but there's no denying, the years are advancing whether I like it or not.

I don't sleep very well. Next door Lizzie always wakes early. Via our party wall I can track her movements: Radio Four News goes on at seven, she gets up at ten past, after the headlines.

I hear her calling the cats in at the kitchen door, then she makes herself tea and takes it back to bed. She doesn't move again till the radio switches off at eight.

There's no point my getting up then in the hope of seeing her. She's completely absorbed in her own world till lunchtime, but during the week I used to be able to depend on meeting her for tea or coffee at least twice. Ideally, I preferred to go to her house because then I could extend my visit. When she visited me, she'd accept a second cup, but after an hour she'd become restless and stop feeding me opening lines that might lead to a lengthier conversation.

Last Christmas morning she asked me over for a sherry and mince pies. There were three cigarette butts in the ashtray so I knew that her friend Jackie had already been in.

Lizzie wore a silky blouse – a Christmas present from her brother and his wife, she said – pale grey with three-quarter length sleeves. She'd spoilt the effect of the low scoop neckline by putting a white tee-shirt underneath.

She seemed moderately pleased with the earrings I'd bought her. Diamante and dangly. Once, when we were getting along better, she told me that her ex-husband always wanted her to wear feminine clothes. Each Christmas or birthday, he'd choose an outfit for her. She said, "He bought them for his own enjoyment rather than mine. He got pleasure seeing me wearing them. It was a control thing."

I nodded sympathetically, but privately I was on the husband's side. The few times I've seen her dressed up for an evening out, she's looked terrific.

I had my glass of sherry and two mince pies, then the telephone in the hall rang and she went to answer it. A Christmas card lay open on the kitchen table. I twisted my head to read the message. "To my darling Lizzie. Love you always. Jackie."

Foolish of me not to have understood how the land lay.

LIZZIE

My neighbour Derek has kept budgerigars for over a quarter of a century. In his back yard there is a wooden aviary he built himself. When I first moved here, I worried that my two cats might prove a problem, but after satisfying some initial curiosity they seemed to understand that the budgerigars behind their expanse of wire mesh were unobtainable.

I'm an early riser but even so, at first, the noise the birds made at dawn woke me. I've got used to their song now. I like it. They chirrup and chatter and sometimes argue. And they're quite beautiful; such a range of blues and greens and yellows.

I once asked Derek which bird was his favourite.

"I don't have favourites," he said. "It's more the process I enjoy."

I must have looked mystified.

"Well Lizzie, I select the pairs and cage the birds up for a week without a nest-box, allowing them to bond. Then I release them into the communal area." He'd grinned. "The cocks might take a look at the other hens, but usually they stick with the partners I've chosen for them."

He'd shown me a clutch of budgerigar eggs; three were white and one was the palest grey. He held them out to me in the palm of his hand. "Guess which one's infertile?"

"The grey one?"

"Correct." He let the grey egg slip through his fingers. It made no sound as it landed on the concrete paving. It didn't shatter, the shell parted into tiny pieces.

*

When Derek first invited me into his house, I noticed a grainy, black and white photograph on his kitchen dresser. It was of his late wife Monica asleep in a deckchair, taken on a Blackpool beach during the 1970s. She was very pretty, her hair worn chin length in loose dark curls. She wore cropped trousers and a tee-shirt. Really, she could have been mistaken for a contemporary woman.

"Of course, Monica didn't look like that by the time she died," Derek said, his tone of voice dismissive. "By then she'd piled on the pounds."

Later, while he waited for the kettle to boil, he showed me another photograph: full colour this time and mounted in a polished silver frame.

"Your wife was very photogenic." I took the photograph over to his kitchen window where the light was better.

"That's Dawn. Monica's daughter by her first husband."

"She looks exactly like her mum."

"I can't see it." He dropped tea bags into two mugs. "Jaffa cake, Lizzie?"

DEREK

In the early days of our friendship, I offered Lizzie a lift in my car to the Selly Oak branch of Sainsbury's, where I do my weekly shop. I was pleasantly surprised when she accepted. It became an enjoyable ritual. We'd start with coffee and a toasted teacake in the cafe before going our separate ways around the store. Because I find it uncomfortable to stand for any length of time (that touch of arthritis in my left knee), she'd queue up while I commandeered a table. I liked the way she organised everything: extra milk and sugar, extra butter and jam. I felt flattered to be fussed over by such an attractive woman; I'd imagine some of the other old codgers in the cafeteria envying my luck.

Afterwards, I'd hurry with my shopping because I didn't want to seem an elderly slow-coach, but every time she'd manage to beat me back to the car. One morning as we piled our shopping into the car boot, I quipped, "We'll have to stop meeting like this."

She gave me a thin, unamused smile to indicate that I'd stepped over a line – drawn, of course, by her. After that, Jackie and her Fiat 500 took over the supermarket run with Lizzie.

LIZZIE

"I was a recidivist," Derek said.

We were standing in his kitchen, waiting for the kettle to boil. "I'm sorry, Derek. What is that?"

He'd looked surprised at my ignorance. "A repeat offender. A jail bird."

"I had no idea."

He put our mugs of tea on a tray. "There came a point when I'd spent more time in prison than out of it."

I followed him into the front room. After almost two years, this had become quite a tiresome habit, every other day, which I was finding hard to avoid. Derek set the tray down on his coffee table. As always, he took the winged armchair while I sat in the corner of the sofa with my back to the window.

He smiled at me. "You look very nice and fresh in that green blouse, Lizzie."

I ignored his compliment. "But wasn't your wife upset?"

"About what?"

"You being in prison all the time."

"Of course she was. Particularly during the first few years. We were quite a passionate couple, although I never could resist a bit on the side." He winked at me. "Have I shocked you, Lizzie?"

"I'm not sure." I wasn't so much shocked by what he'd said as the casual way he'd said it. "Not much of a life for Monica."

As if I'd missed a crucial point, he frowned. "I might not have been any great shakes as a husband, but there were far worse."

"So, what did you go to prison for?"

"Fraud. A white-collar crime for a blue-collar worker. Not everyone can say that. Pass my tea." He'd looked pleased with himself, even proud.

I could see why employers would trust Derek. My therapist would describe him as 'grounded'. He's quite tall and well built. Even with his gammy knee, he looks like he'd be a handy chap to have on your side in a fight. His voice as well – it has that Brummie lilt that I find almost comforting. I'd trust Derek. I *did* trust him. He had a set of keys to my house for when I was away.

"I liked office work," he continued. "Somehow within a very short time, I'd be put in charge of the petty cash or the Christmas fund. I have an aptitude for figures so I took a course in book-keeping. I was able to go for bigger and better jobs: invoice clerk, accounts manager." He leant towards me and picked a tuft of cat fur from the knee of my trousers. "As sure as night followed day, eventually they'd cotton on. Possibly I wanted to be found out. You won't like this, but I got a buzz from watching their faces when they realised I'd taken them in. It's quite a powerful position, to be able to destroy someone's confidence in their own judgement, don't you think?"

I answered Derek's question with one of my own. "How did you keep getting work?"

"Forged references." His expression was wolfish. "In those days, the more impressive your reference, the less chance they'd bother to check up on you."

"And did you always cheat?"

"I didn't cheat. It was fraud. A proper crime." He shrugged. "Sometimes an employer turned out to be too nice to do the dirty on. But then I'd get bored and hand in my notice. You see, my day-to-day siphoning off of even small sums of cash made working for someone else bearable. Something to get out of bed for."

DEREK

I wonder if Lizzie's punishing me for overstepping the mark a few weeks ago. She'd called in for a cup of coffee. She was wearing smart black jeans and a white polo-neck. The jumper had a snowflake pattern on it which suited her *and* the weather, which had turned wintry.

She told me that in the afternoon she was going to watch Jackie sing in the Victorian Tea Rooms in Kings Heath Park.

I said, "It's a rotten day, I'll drive you down. I could come along and take photographs."

Up till the moment I said that, Lizzie had been cheerful and relaxed, but then a familiar barrier dropped between us.

"Really, Derek, there's no need," she said quickly.

"My dear, it's pouring with rain and very cold."

I could see the 'my dear' rankled. I saw a flash of anger in her eyes before she said, "Thank you, Derek. That's kind of you."

At two fifty-five I knocked on our party wall. By then, the sleet-filled rain had stopped. We emerged from our separate houses at exactly the same moment. When she saw the pullover I was wearing, she frowned. It was a polo-neck, navy blue with a white snowflake pattern, very similar in style to hers.

We drove in silence. The atmosphere in the car was so

tense I missed the park entrance and was forced to pull in quite some distance up the road. In single file we walked for a quarter of a mile along a narrow path of sodden leaves.

"This will give us a bit of exercise. We should get more fresh air," I said as if she, like me, spent most of her days indoors. Again, I sensed how much she disliked my use of 'us' and 'we' as if we were a couple.

By the time we reached the tearooms, Jackie was already there, sitting at a table. Seeing our pullovers, she laughed. "The two of you look as if you've been on an alpine holiday together."

Lizzie didn't smile, she looked annoyed. "If I'd known Derek was wearing a similar jumper today, I would have changed."

"Well I'm so glad you didn't." With a gallant flourish I pulled out a chair for her. "My lady," I said.

She ignored the chair. "I'm ordering a sandwich and a hot chocolate," she said and walked away towards the counter.

"Can I get you anything, Derek?" Jackie asked.

I shook my head. "I'm fine."

LIZZIE

I only found out recently that Derek's wife committed suicide. He mentioned it quite casually one afternoon as he poured boiling water over our tea bags.

"Didn't I tell you?" he asked.

"No Derek, you didn't."

"In this house. Sleeping pills and vodka. Dawn, her daughter, found her."

"I'm so sorry. It must have been devastating for Dawn."

"It was, although she was a pretty game girl."

"Was?"

We Share a Party Wall

"Was – is. She lived here for a time but then she began a relationship with a man she'd met at work and I chucked her out."

"That was harsh."

"I wasn't having the two of them canoodling under my roof."

"No. I see that," I said. "I'm sorry about your wife. How tragic."

"Is it? Isn't it just life?"

"It isn't like anything in my life."

"What, nobody's committed suicide, had affairs, been dishonest?"

"Possibly. But once or twice removed, never people I was close to."

"Take out the tea bags," Derek instructed as he opened a fresh bottle of milk.

I noticed that he'd moved the photographs of mother and daughter next to each other. They looked the same age – still young – decades younger than me.

We trooped into his front room. Derek sat very straight backed in his usual chair, the fingers of his right hand drumming the chair arm as if in time to some inner music. That afternoon we didn't find much to say to one another. To relieve the silence, I told him about a building site next to the railway station, the two gigantic cranes silhouetted against the sky, the way they dwarfed the surrounding houses. "Derek, the cranes would make a brilliant photograph."

He answered, "To change the subject ever so slightly, I've never told anyone all this stuff about my life before. There's something about you that makes it easy to spill the beans."

I didn't want there to be something about me. The room felt hot and closed in. It was tidy but dust lay on every surface:

the bookshelves, the television, the magazines arranged into neat piles that had never looked disturbed in all the months I'd been coming in.

I stood up. "Better get on, Jackie will be over soon."

He leaned forward, "Are you frightened of men, Lizzie?"

"No Derek, they're just not my cup of tea." I smiled and raised my empty mug.

DEREK

I did not see Lizzie for several days following the pullover incident, but then she came in bringing a box of lemon curd tarts from the local shop. I didn't really want cakes because they represent one more temptation. These last few months I've put on half a stone. I can't seem to stop eating. It's because I'm dissatisfied. Each day stretches out, my happiness dependent on glimpsing Lizzie.

We ate the tarts. Licking her fingers, she said, "Lemon curd is delicious, but not so delicious I could eat a whole jar."

I showed her a project I'd started, a catalogue of my birds: their names, bloodlines, size, colour, competitions – win and place – all with individual photographs. I'd had the devil of a job isolating each one to take the picture. Budgerigars being social birds, they hadn't liked it one little bit!

"These photographs are extraordinary," she said. "Such detail. Budgies have such intelligent bright eyes – or is that just your clever photography? Derek, I'm impressed."

"Compliments indeed." My voice was gruff as I tried to hide how pleased I felt at her approval. "Perhaps you'll be interested in these as well," I said.

I got down on my hands and knees and dragged my leather portfolio of table-top photographs from under the sofa – not of budgerigars, but of weird and wonderful objects I've collected over the years.

"Ah, you showed me those once before," she said.

"There are a few new photographs I'd like your opinion on."

I'd added two self-portraits. I thought I looked quite impressive, my expression thoughtful, gaze penetrating – a cross between Ernest Hemingway and Sigmund Freud. The photographs were monochrome, which tends to make faces look younger, and I must admit I'd Photoshopped some of the lines on my forehead and the ones running down from my nostrils to my chin.

"You look most handsome," she said in a bright, false voice, as if she was unwillingly judging a best baby competition.

"Do you really think so?"

"I wouldn't say anything I didn't mean." She picked up one of the photos. "Yes, I like this one the best. There's more light and shade."

I didn't want to hear about light and shade. "Would you go out with someone who looked like that?"

She appeared puzzled, but I knew she understood exactly what I was saying. "Derek, as you well know, I don't go out with men."

"Yes, but you used to. You told me you were married once. What about then?"

"That was a long time ago."

"Yes or no?" I'd never snapped at her before, but I felt utterly desperate to have some recognition of me as a man.

She answered quietly as if she was trying to calm me down. "I'm sorry, Derek, but of course my answer's 'no'."

"Suit yourself," I snarled.

Another puzzled look. "You do know that Jackie is my girlfriend?"

"Girlfriend?" I filled my voice with sneering amusement. "As in?"

"That's enough," she said.

We sat in silence. My photos, scattered across the carpet, were now an embarrassment, but I couldn't bring myself to gather them up in front of her. Then, very slowly, my lounge door opened. It was one of her cats. He looked uncertain until he saw her sitting on my sofa. He hurried over and jumped onto her lap.

We both laughed. It cleared the air, I think.

"You must have left your kitchen window open," she said. "I'd better take him home."

"No hurry."

But she was on the move. The barrier was back in place.

I heard a snatch of news through the wall this morning. Israeli war planes were attacking the Gaza Strip. News like that, world news, means nothing to me anymore.

From next door came the sound of Lizzie opening her bedroom window to let in the sharp fresh air. I know what her bedroom looks like. In the past when she's been away, I've looked in all the rooms. Downstairs, she has a lot of colour: pictures, cushions, pink and green fairy lights looped around the living-room door frame. Upstairs the two bedrooms are painted white. Pale green carpet, white blinds, everything neat and somehow very still.

I've sat on the edge of her bed. (I factor Jackie out because she doesn't live with Lizzie, she has her own house fifty yards away.) I've smelt Lizzie's pillows. I don't have the words to describe how her pillows smell, how that scent makes me feel. I've tried to imagine myself as a fixture in her bedroom. To be honest, this doesn't work. Even wearing new pyjamas, I can't see myself fitting in. And definitely not naked. I'd be like a worn-out old dog that had first rolled in mud. I would be unpleasantly inappropriate within Lizzie's perfect setting.

'Inappropriate' is one of *her* words. She used to tell me about friends' 'inappropriate behaviour'. Then she'd smile and apologise for using 'jargon'. I've looked that word up and yes, she does use jargon. I'd sit and listen, watch her face, the way she smiled, or chuckled, or seemed anxious, but often what she had to say was quite banal.

LIZZIE

I decided to break the pattern of tea with Derek several afternoons a week. I considered talking to Jackie but really what could I say? *He makes me feel uneasy.*

Annoyingly, I felt sorry for him. From behind my bedroom blinds I'd look down into his garden, watching as he pottered about inside and outside the aviary. He never spoke to his birds, never tried to make a connection with them. Every few minutes he'd glance hopefully over the wall towards my closed patio doors.

After a week, I gave in – I couldn't spend the rest of my life indoors avoiding his company, but I would at least try to arrange our meetings on my terms. A mild Wednesday morning arrived. I went into the garden. Within seconds, Derek's back door opened and out he came, humming, as if he had no idea I was there.

"Would you like to pop in for tea and cake this afternoon?" I called out.

"I didn't see you there, Lizzie." He pretended to look amazed. "I was just about to put the kettle on myself, you could come in for tea now."

"I'm waiting for a parcel delivery."

"Leave a note on the front door."

"I'd rather not. It's quite an important parcel and I still have some work to finish. About three?"

By three o'clock I was ready. I'd exchanged my usual mugs for cups and saucers and arranged an assortment of cakes on a plate. We sat at the kitchen table, facing the patio doors so we could look out over my garden.

"You keep it nice," he said.

"Thank you." I began to pour boiling water into the teapot.

"It's not that different from how it was when Dawn lived here."

"Your stepdaughter?" I looked up and some of the water spilt onto the tablecloth. "She lived in *my* house?"

"Before your time, the two houses formed one large house. Where your oven is now, there was a door that led into my hallway. Dawn had a small studio up in your second bedroom. She painted. Not very well."

I stirred the tea and began to pour.

He gave me an amused look. "Very ladylike."

"You do things your way," I said evenly. "I do things mine."

"I *thought* you were trying to tell me something like that." He paused. "The upper landing ran right across between our two houses."

"Did it? How long ago did all this happen?" I asked.

"All what?"

"Well... when was the house divided up?"

"Monica died five years ago, Dawn left a year later, and then the house was altered."

I saved this up to consider later and said, "It must still be very painful for you."

"Some of it is. After my wife died, I expected life to improve."

He reached for a jam tart, took a bite. Crumbs missed the

We Share a Party Wall

plate and showered onto his lap. He brushed them to the floor.

"In what way improve?"

"Use your imagination, Lizzie."

I looked down at the crumbs. Whether Derek realised it or not, we had reached an impasse. I said, "My imagination tells me you were having an affair with your wife's daughter. You thought that with Monica out of the picture, you and Dawn could continue without any interference. Perhaps you even imagined that eventually the two of you would get married."

"Yes," he said, "That's about right. I focus on what I want and usually I get it."

I ignored him. "I think once her mum was dead, Dawn didn't want you."

He smiled so I could see his teeth. Good, strong teeth, but yellowing.

"I bet she felt guilty and found herself not able to stand the sight of you. Am I right, Derek? Is that the real reason she took up with the new boyfriend you told me about?"

He reached for another cake, his hand shook slightly. "From the moment Dawn discovered Monica was dead, she turned on me. It broke my heart."

"*Poor you*," I said, my voice full of dislike.

DEREK

Today was my birthday. Lizzie came in with a present and card. She did telephone earlier to see if I was up. I wasn't, but I said I was.

"Give me ten minutes," I told her.

She gave me fifteen.

It was only as I opened the door that I realised what filthy old clothes I'd pulled on. She leant towards me but then took a step back, as if she'd geared herself up to give me a birthday peck on the cheek but suddenly thought better of it. Instead she whisked past and marched into my front room.

"Cup of tea?" I said, trying to keep the desperation from my voice.

"Off to Solihull in ten minutes. I just popped in to say Happy Birthday. So glad you were up and at 'em."

"I've been awake hours. I'm wearing my old clothes because I thought I'd make a start on painting the front room."

She looked relieved. "Well don't work too hard. You should do something nice. Dinner with your family perhaps?"

"Perhaps. Don't let me keep you." With feigned disinterest I dropped her present and card onto my coffee table.

"I'll be home around six tomorrow. I've left extra food for the cats. No need to feed them." She gave me a brief, apologetic smile. "Sorry, but I'd better rush."

"Yes, you'd better."

I sat in the armchair for most of the day, watching programme after programme of meaningless television. Her present lay in its torn wrapping paper on the coffee table; her card – a drawing of an elderly man relaxing in a deck chair as if his life was over – on the mantelpiece. The present was a box of Turkish Delight. I've seen them – two for the price of one – in the supermarket.

Saturday

LIZZIE

I had no intention of going to Solihull. I went to stay with Jackie for the night. Did I set a test for Derek? Well, yes, I did. Once or twice, I've sensed that in my absence, Derek has been in my upstairs rooms. Jackie would have accused me of having an overactive imagination, but after listening to Derek's stories

We Share a Party Wall

about his life, I needed to be sure that he was trustworthy.

This morning just after nine I quietly let myself back into my house. Everything was exactly as I'd left it. Some of the anxiety I've been feeling around Derek slipped from my shoulders. Then from above, I heard a floorboard creak.

I made no sound climbing the stairs. Before I went away, I'd shut my bedroom door, but as I reached the landing, I saw that it was wide open. A square of sunlight from the dormer window fell on the carpet, where Derek sat, one leg tucked under, his bad leg stretched out. He turned his head to face me. His chest was bare. Beside him, folded neatly, lay his shirt and vest. His skin was grey and white, as if dust had settled between the creases.

I wasn't frightened – I felt embarrassed, catching him out like this. "Derek, what are you doing up here?" I disliked my tone of voice; I sounded imperious, as if our twenty-year age difference was the deciding factor as to where the power lay.

"Thinking," he said.

"I'd rather you thought in your own house."

"You remind me of Dawn." He waved one hand. "This room, it's just how she had it: pale colours, pretty pictures on the walls, a kimono dressing gown on the back of the door."

"I'm going downstairs now," I said gently. "Get dressed and go home."

"You don't like me anymore, do you? At first you did. I should have kept quiet."

"Derek, I never liked you in the way you mean. I never could have."

Sitting at the kitchen table. I waited. Five full minutes passed before I heard Derek's footsteps on the stairs, then in the hall. My front door opening and closing. The letterbox flipped open and my set of keys dropped to the floor.

DEREK

I've been in love before. What I mean is I'm capable of love. I loved my wife, at least for the first few years of our marriage. I loved her daughter, Dawn. What I feel for Lizzie is very different. Whatever this feeling is, it hurts like hell. If I was close enough to anyone in this world to be able to ask them, *"What can I do?"*, they would no doubt advise, "Give it up, man. Right from the get-go, you never stood a chance with her. You have adjoining houses. You share a party wall, end of story!"

A DAY SPENT WITH DEIRDRE

It is ten o'clock on Saturday morning and I've agreed to go to Bluewater with Deirdre. As we're about to set off, her partner Martin – wearing pyjamas and a shabby dressing gown – comes down from the loft room. Deirdre calls this room Martin's 'sleep/work station'. She has explained that Martin is a 'night person' who does most of his work after dark. Rather than wake her up (they no longer share a bedroom) he sleeps on a futon in the loft.

"Sweet cheeks," she calls out. Martin winces. "There's a new box of that zillion-seed Granola you like for breakfast."

"Any bread?" he asks. "I need a tuna and mayo infusion."

Deirdre throws me a mock despairing look. "What can you do with him?"

I collude and also shrug my shoulders in mock despair.

Deirdre produces a baguette, tips a tin of tuna into a bowl and squirts on mayonnaise.

"More mayo," he says.

Again, she looks at me. "He really shouldn't."

If it were any of my business, I'd tell her, "Deirdre, Martin's supposed to be your partner, not your badly behaved teenage son. He's fifty this year and incapable of even changing his own underwear unless you indicate that a clean pair is required!" But it isn't any of my business, and although Deirdre likes to complain about Martin, she would not appreciate any criticism coming from me.

Martin settles with his baguette on their white leather sofa and switches on the TV. Their cat, Lord Dudley, emerges from behind a cushion and joins him. Lord Dudley's bright blue eyes, which are startlingly similar to Deirdre's bright blue eyes, fix on the tuna dripping from between the bread.

I arrived at Deirdre's (I never include Martin in the ownership of the house) at nine thirty as requested. I have now been standing with my hand on the front door knob for over half an hour.

Finally, Deirdre throws her pashmina about her shoulders and grabs car keys and purse. She hesitates.

I sigh.

"Got change for the Dartford Tunnel, lover?"

Martin chokes angrily on the baguette.

While having little sympathy for him, I do think it is perverse of Deirdre to litter their communications with endearments when he so clearly dislikes them. If someone winced or choked each time I called them 'sweet cheeks' or 'lover', I'd desist pretty quickly.

Martin looks expectantly at me.

"I've only got my credit card," I say quickly. I do have a twenty-pound note in the back pocket of my jeans, but I have no intention of disclosing that. Martin and Deirdre have a way of getting through my money with ease. They have never understood the concept of 'paying back' and they probably owe me somewhere in the region of a thousand pounds.

As if he's exhausted and hasn't spent at least twelve hours in bed, Martin slumps against the sofa cushions. "I do have change," he says. "But it's up top."

A Day Spent with Deirdre

"Could you get it?" Deirdre asks.

"I could but I don't want to. The tunnel takes credit cards."

"Sweet pea, I seem to remember that the tunnel doesn't take credit cards. Of course, I could be wrong."

"You are wrong."

Deirdre only ever looks anxious around Martin. Everyone else and she goes from a standing start of being pleasant and cheerful to a full-scale tornado of fury. "But just in case I'm right."

Martin rallies. He sits up and takes another bite of his baguette. "Don't be ridiculous, Deirdre. This is the twenty-first century. Every Joe Bloggs takes credit cards."

As we finally drive off Deirdre asks, "Who or what is Joe Bloggs?"

"I think it's a chain of shoe shops," I answer.

At the Dartford Tunnel, we find a long queue of cars, aggravated by everyone fishing in their wallets, pockets and glove compartments for change. Deirdre winds down her window and starts humming 'You're So Vain', keeping time with her credit card against the car door.

Finally, we reach the head of the line and approach the payment kiosk. She offers the tunnel attendant her most radiant and apologetic smile. "I'm so sorry. I left my change purse on the draining board at home, all I've got is my credit card."

"We don't take credit cards," man says pleasantly enough.

"Oh, surely you do."

"No, surely we don't. Cash only."

Deirdre changes tactic, switching to her most imperious tone. "Look here, I'm certain the last time I came through, you accepted my credit card. After all, this is the twenty-first century. Even Joe Bloggs accepts them."

"I'm not Joe Bloggs."

Behind us someone hits their horn, which is immediately taken up by other drivers.

Deirdre says, "I remember it was early December and I was driving up to John Lewis's to do a spot of Christmas shopping."

The attendant smiles slightly.

Deirdre relaxes and smiles back at him.

I smile too, although I do feel guilty with the twenty-pound note burning a hole in my pocket.

The attendant leans out through the kiosk window and looks down at Deirdre. His smile broadens. He is going to give Deirdre the benefit of the doubt and let the car through.

"You're a ruddy little liar," he says.

Deirdre recoils as if she's been struck.

The man hasn't finished. "Now if you don't have the money to pay, I'll close this lane and call the police."

"But I don't have the money, nor does my friend. My partner Martin insisted that you took credit cards."

"Then your partner Martin doesn't know his arse from his elbow." He picks up a phone.

"What if I give you my name and address?"

He shakes his head and speaks into his mobile. "I've got two women in a blue Audi with no money. Okay. Will do."

Within a matter of seconds, the traffic police arrive. Behind us the line of cars is filtered into the next lane, everyone staring out of their windows at us as if we might be a couple of apprehended bank robbers.

A police car pulls up next to us. The driver waves his hand out of the window signalling for us to follow. We drive down a ramp and into a large enclosure. On three sides, there are high brick walls with barbed wire running along the top.

The policeman gets out of his car. He pats the truncheon

A Day Spent with Deirdre

hanging from his leather belt as if reassuring himself that he has it, and then saunters towards us. He is tall, well built and intimidating.

So far, I haven't shown myself up in any heroic light. Had I just proffered my twenty-pound note, we would have been well on our way to Bluewater by now. I lean across Deirdre and shout though her open window, "Officer, this is ludicrous!"

The officer alters direction, from Deirdre's car door to mine. He peers in at me. "You think this is ludicrous, do you?" His voice is silky.

I am remembering the film *Dirty Harry*, where the silky-voiced cop produces a Smith and Wesson .44 Magnum revolver and blasts off the kneecap of a fugitive from justice after very little provocation. I tense my legs to stop my quivering kneecaps drawing attention to themselves. "Ludicrous wasn't quite the word I was looking for," I respond weakly.

Next to me, Deirdre takes a deep breath. I know her so well. She is not worrying about blasted kneecaps; she is building up to an almighty temper tantrum.

"Let's get this straight," she says. "We are only talking about one pound and fifty pence?"

"One pound and fifty pence that neither of you have," the cop says. "Do you know how many times a week some Johnny tries to get through this tunnel without paying?"

In my head, the film has changed to a prisoner-of-war escape movie...

"No idea," Deirdre says, and tosses her hair as if she couldn't care less.

Cop tucks one hand into his belt loop and begins to rock back and forth on his heels. "At least twice every week."

He announces this as if expecting us to be impressed – we are not.

Deirdre makes a quick mental arithmetic calculation. "That's only one hundred and fifty-six pounds a year. Hardly a major crime!"

"But it is a crime," he says.

"*But not a major one*, which means," Deirdre pauses for effect, "it's a tiny little misdemeanour."

The cop has had enough. "How would you like to spend the next couple of days in a prison cell?"

"What! For not coughing up a measly one pound fifty?" she roars back at him.

"No. For lying, cheating, and arguing with a police officer."

"Look dude –" she begins.

As much as I admire Deirdre's feisty spirit, I don't want to end the day in a cell. I grab her arm and hiss, "Keep quiet. I'll deal with this."

"That's right, lady – you tell her."

I think I've now gone some way to winning the policeman round. He is grinning and obviously quite enjoying the altercation.

"I'm really sorry about this misunderstanding. Maybe I can sort…" I begin to search my pockets, search mythical pockets, till finally I withdraw my twenty-pound note from the back pocket of my jeans and flourish it.

Deirdre grabs my arm, "No way! We're not paying. I'd rather go to jail!"

I hand him the note. "It may be a little faded, officer – must have gone through the wash. I had no idea it was there."

The policeman walks back towards the kiosk, returning five minutes later with my change and a ticket. He says, "We've got the details of this car on file. If either of you try this stunt again, you'll be in big trouble. Understand?"

"She understands, officer," I say.

A Day Spent with Deirdre

"I'm talking to you too."

"Fair enough."

Deirdre revs the car engine impatiently. We leave the enclosure and join the line of traffic. At the kiosk, we show our ticket and are allowed through. Ten minutes later we are back on track.

I wait for Deirdre to say something, to vent some of her anger on me. She is silent until we pull in at Bluewater. She unfastens her seat belt but makes no attempt to reach for her shoulder bag.

"This has all been Martin's fault," she says. "He wanted me out of the house so he could go back to bed, or do whatever he does when I'm not there. I've been set up. Thrown to the lions."

"That's a bit extreme..."

She turns towards me. "Think about it. Martin's a man."

I nod agreement.

"He knows stuff about tunnel charges. Of course they don't want to be faffing around with credit cards for one pound fifty. He was happy for me to get arrested, rather than go up two flights of stairs and find his money."

"Deirdre, he's just lazy. And he knows you can look after yourself."

"What if I can't? What would have happened if you hadn't found that twenty?"

"The policeman wouldn't have arrested two women over such a small amount. He was just trying to intimidate us."

"Well, he didn't intimidate me!"

"No, he didn't. And well done you! But that just proves my point – you can take care of yourself."

She looks thoughtful. "Perhaps in the future, I should pretend that I can't take care of myself."

"Pretending is never a good idea. Come on, Deirdre, let's not spoil the day."

She plays with the silky fringe of her pashmina. "Bottom line – Martin doesn't love me anymore. Probably never did."

"Now that is ludicrous. He adores the ground you walk on."

But of course, he doesn't. Martin is very fond of Deirdre but he adores himself. I've always known that.

We enter Bluewater shopping mall. With manic determination, Deirdre spends five hundred pounds on clothes, all of which she refuses to try on first. I know she is upset and that her day out has been ruined, although on the drive home she insists that she is thrilled with every item purchased.

"They represent a new me for summer," she says. "And the peignoir's fabulous for weekend lounging."

The following morning, she rings early. Her voice is artificially bright: "I'm taking the lot back, except the peignoir. Want to come?"

I can't face another long car journey with a manic Deirdre. "Not today, Deirdre. I'm up to my eyes." There is silence on the line. "Are you okay?" I ask.

"I'm fine," she says. In the background I hear Martin mutter something. "Sorry, sweet cheeks," she calls out to him. "You want a chip butty?" And Deirdre puts the phone down.

THE TIME OF THEIR LIVES

I

Friends & Family

I'm sitting on my bed, a dog-eared copy of Noel Streatfeild's *Tennis Shoes* open on my lap. Outside I hear a car reversing into our one-way street, the tick-tock of its indicators, the complaint of brakes and then the car door slamming, followed by laughing voices. Book dropping to the floor, I rush across to the window. Down below, two women are smiling and waving. Both are tall and very blonde with frosted pink lips. They wear identical trouser suits, except one is navy, the other a pale blue that perfectly matches their smart Morris Minor convertible. Their jackets are fitted with wide buckled belts cinched in to make their waists seem tiny.

My mother, dressed more sombrely in a demure Courtelle twin-set and black stretch slacks, comes into view. "You found us then?" she says.

In unison the women shout as they hug her, "Oh, bless you, Dot – no trouble at all! Took us fifteen minutes door to door. The chocolates? They're for you of course, you daft so-and-so!"

Upstairs in our rented furnished flat, I move away from the window and go out onto the landing. I stare into the gloomy sitting room. What will these glamorous women think of the dark heavy furniture? The Victorian sideboard is massive, rising six feet high, topped with the carved head and outspread wings of an eagle; our cumbersome bookcases are packed with dusty hardbacked books that we have never opened. All the property of Mrs Storey, our landlady. Nothing is ours apart from a few cushions and the television.

I needn't have worried. The twins love everything, even me!

Still laughing and shouting, they tumble into the hall. Mrs Storey emerges from her kitchen to see what all the noise is about.

"Just a couple of my friends," Mum says, tossing her head and adopting a haughty tone of voice intended to put Mrs Storey firmly in her place.

Feeling shy but curious, I remain on the landing as Mum leads the twins around the bend in the stairs.

"And this is my daughter," Mum says. "Cathy, meet the twins."

The twins look up at me, their faces breaking into expressions of delight.

"The little love," they yell.

"More a bloody nuisance," Mum says, sourly but with no real malice.

They envelop me in their arms and cover my face with wet pink kisses. Unused to such physical displays of affection, I fight the desire to wipe their kisses away.

"How old is she? Nine! Dot, you have to be joking! Never in a million years! She'd pass for a young teenager. She's so much like you. Particularly around the eyes. You don't think so? Whatever, she's a pet. We love her, don't we, Lesley?"

Friends & Family

"We do. We love the little sweetheart!"

Never in my young life has anyone loved me on sight. In those first moments I give up my heart. I ache to share everything about myself with them and bask in the warmth of their affectionate attention, and I am so happy that my brother Steven is away in boarding school and not here to hog the limelight.

Mum turns to me. "Drinks please."

I fix their gin and tonics, Mum's Campari and lemonade. I bring in crisps and refill the bowl several times. I sit at their feet and adore them. They ask me about school, about boys, what do I want to be when I grow up?

"A dress designer," I say. "Like Mary Quant."

"Bless her!" they shout. In the space of an hour they bless me at least a dozen times. When the hour is up, I refuse to go to bed, till Mum loses her temper.

"Get to bed – right now!"

The twins look regretful. "Ah, the little sweetheart," they say. "Love her to bits!"

Once in bed, I find it difficult to fall asleep. In the next room I hear their voices rising and falling like music. Hardly a word from Mum, but then her voice is always quiet.

"Perfectly modulated," is Mum's description.

Instead of counting sheep, I fall asleep listing possible compliments they might be giving Mum, all about me, with the words 'love' or 'lovely' or 'bless' included somewhere in the sentence.

My mother works in London for a solicitor, which is where she met Lesley and Jean. Just before the previous Christmas they joined as secretarial temps. At first Mum hated them. She said they were loud, brash, common, on the hunt for rich husbands. Mum didn't like women, particularly younger women; Jean and Lesley were in their late twenties, while she was nearing forty. However, in spite of Mum's hostility, the twins took to her.

"They think I'm hilarious," Mum told me one evening, looking reluctantly pleased. "I try to tell them that I'm being perfectly serious, they *are* incompetent, *do* have deafening voices, dress inappropriately, flirt with anything in trousers – but they laugh as if I've said something incredibly funny. Not in a nasty way. They seem to find me endearing. I'm beginning to warm to them, particularly Lesley – she's not quite as loud as Jean."

The twins moved on to another job in Bishopsgate. Mum said, "It's so quiet in the office. I miss them. Everybody does."

We both thought that would be the end of any friendship, but within a week Lesley had rung her up. The three of them met for lunch and then other lunches and sometimes after-work drinks in the bar at Liverpool Street Station. Instead of complaints about her train journey home or how many letters she's been obliged to type that day, Mum starts bringing back stories of the twins' adventures abroad, that they've been engaged to be married at least four times each. I am entranced.

Lesley and Jean are identical twins and were indistinguishable as children, but now, nearing thirty, there are subtle differences. However, it still takes three visits to our flat for me to work out who is who. Lesley is my favourite. She is prettier than Jean and fragile looking. She suffers from diabetes. Each day she gives herself an insulin injection. In her handbag she carries a bar of Cadbury's chocolate in case her sugar level drops. Often, at the end of an evening, she will leave the chocolate behind for me.

"Plenty more bars at home, Dot," I hear her say one evening when I'm supposedly asleep in my bed. "The little one needs feeding up." I am tall for my age and awkward. I warm to being thought of as a 'little one'.

Jean is very different. She *is* noisy and brash, always restless, never still. If I go on too long with an anguished tale of school life, she'll suddenly cut across me with a sharp, "For god's sake, give it a rest. Nothing's the end of the world, surely, lovey?"

She is never sharp with Mum. They both think the world of Mum, that she is very brave to have taken her two children and fled from a wicked husband. Their eyes fill with tears when she shows them my brother's letters sent from boarding school.

"It's heartbreaking," Jean says at least once during each visit. "A mother parted from her son. Your ex should be hung, drawn and quartered!"

The twins tell Mum everything that happens in their lives. When she is with them, Mum is at her best. I make myself as innocuous as possible because I don't want to be packed off to bed and this way I'm able to observe everyone. I see how a light switches on inside my mother when they arrive and switches off at the end of the evening. I see that she tries her best to appear carefree and happy. I see the strain in her face sometimes and know that the effort she has to make, to be other than she is, exhausts her.

The twins live five miles away with their parents and one brother. There is another older brother, Theo, living in New Zealand. Although they talk fondly about Theo, it is as if he is dead or at least of no consequence. The brother living at home, Jimmy, is ten years their senior. Mum says that men of thirty-eight shouldn't be living in a boxroom at their parents' house.

Mum tells me that when Jimmy was nineteen, he was arrested for accosting a younger lad in a public toilet. The twins insist that it was all a terrible mistake. The incident never went to trial but the trauma made Jimmy withdraw from the world. In the middle of Mum recounting this highly interesting story, she suddenly stops and says fiercely, "You must never repeat this to another living soul!"

Jimmy is a gardener now for the council, even though he doesn't like gardening.

"It gets him out of the house," Lesley says. "He loves the fresh air."

Each week the twins tell us many stories of Jimmy's skills. They idolise this brother. He puts up shelves, hangs doors, asphalts the front drive, in fact does everything a 'real man' should do. He's taken on many of these tasks because their dad is dying slowly of emphysema.

"Jimmy's a marvel with his hands," Jean says... well, shouts.

"Love his heart!" from Lesley.

Due to their father's illness we are never invited to their house, so a routine develops with the twins visiting us every Thursday evening when they are in England. For eight months of each year they take on temp work and then, during the remaining summer months, they tour Italy by car. They love Italian men and Italian men love them. Without fail – bar one occasion – they return home tanned and overflowing with stories of their romantic encounters. Summer brings a new fiancé for each, as if fiancés are lining up in Italy waiting to take their turn.

"Oh, yours was smashing, Jean. I could marry him myself. Mine wasn't such a looker, but charming."

"A lovely man, though. Mario adored Lesley. Didn't he

adore you, darling? Do you remember that time when he broke into our apartment and you'd just gone to bed with your curlers in and he was kissing along the inside of your bare arm and all you could think of was getting rid of those curlers?"

The twins are almost too funny, so that after a while my laughter becomes painful, as if some laughter organ inside my stomach is being stretched further than it can safely go.

As years pass, Mum doesn't always find their company quite so amusing. Sometimes she looks tired quite early in the evening. She gulps her Campari quickly now and instructs me to go easy on the lemonade and not drown it. Once, after they've gone, she is washing glasses and plates while I dry, and I ask her, "Don't you like the twins anymore?"

She doesn't answer immediately, then says with that awful bitterness in her voice that I dread hearing, "I love them but week after week hearing about *their* exploits, *their* relationships and *their* plans for yet another holiday doesn't make me feel any happier about *my* miserable life. Any money they earn, they can spend on themselves; free bed and board, a father, mother and brother who idolise them."

"But they're so full of fun."

"I'd be full of fun, if I was free as a bird." She wrenches out the sink plug and the soapy water swirls away.

Years pass. I am seventeen and studying for my A levels. My brother lives in London now. My parents finally divorce and, with the money Mum receives in the settlement, she is able to buy a semi-detached house in what she describes as 'a better road'. For a few months she seems content. Spurred on by the twins' continuing romantic good fortunes, she places an advert in the personal column of our local paper. We spend an evening constructing it, debating whether or not she can still be classed as 'attractive' and whether she will seem mercenary to aspire to a man with money. Finally, we agree on: *Attractive lady, early forties* (she is now fifty) *would like to meet solvent gentleman aged forty to sixty for intelligent conversation and maybe something more.*

There is one reply, a man called Herbert Jennings who encloses a photograph of his head and shoulders. Mum says he resembles a cadaver but beggars can't be choosers. A tall waxen-faced man in a black shiny suit arrives to escort her to the cinema. Mum takes exception to the suit immediately and also to the ring he wears on his little finger, which is gold-coloured with a large ruby-red stone. She later refers to it as a 'pinky ring' and tells me that men who wear such rings are not to be relied on.

Just after ten thirty that evening I hear their footsteps on the front path and the rustle of Mum foraging for the door key in her handbag.

Mum says, "Herbert, I'm afraid it's rather late to ask you in."

He replies, "I'll just see you settled indoors."

"Well, if you must." Mum unlocks the front door.

As they walk in, I look up from my work. "How was the film?"

"Dreadful," Mum says.

"*Dr Strangelove* is possibly more of a man's film," Herbert says with a horrible smile, as if he already knows Mum hates and despises him.

"Peter Sellers must be my least favourite male film star apart from Burt Lancaster." Mum looks at me. "Can you see Herbert out? I must take a couple of codeine for my headache."

Mum does see him once more, on the bus with a woman old enough to be his mother.

"Perhaps she *was* his mother?" I say.

"I don't think you'd kiss your mother like that," Mum answers – and then, suddenly irritated, "But what do I know?"

The twins, full of noisy enthusiasm, are almost ready to set off to Italy. They have exchanged their Morris Minor for a brand-new bottle-green Citroen 2CV, which is loaded with clothes, and hair and beauty products. They have a list of telephone numbers to ring when they arrive, old fiancés to catch up with, new ones to find. These engagements now seem more a formality than romantic – a necessary requirement if their holiday is to be a success. How would it be if one summer they failed to secure a fiancé? Or worse, just one twin got her man?

Often on Thursday evenings they set up a screen in front of our fireplace and show us black and white slides taken on other holidays going back over ten years. Here are the twins – much younger – in someone's sports car, blonde hair escaping from a scarf tied *à la* Audrey Hepburn; 'the girls', as Mum still calls them, arm-in-arm with tanned handsome dark-haired men who resemble the film star Dirk Bogarde.

But even I – who love the twins so desperately – am growing cynical. One Saturday morning, while Mum and I sit at the kitchen table with coffees, Mum writing out her shopping list, I say, "They're never going to get married, are they?"

She doesn't look up. "Nope."

"Then why do they bother to get engaged?"

"Excitement. The romance of it all. Most of these men want Italian wives who'll settle down in Italy and turn into their mothers. Jean and Lesley will become fond memories of their younger selves. Spaghetti or baked beans?"

"Spaghetti please. But do you think the twins still believe that one day an engagement will turn into marriage?"

Mum chews the end of her biro. "I think Jean still hopes but Lesley's tired of going abroad every year. She's not interested in marriage. She goes to keep her sister company because, whatever Jean says, she'd feel like a fish out of water, wandering around Italy on her own."

It is so rare that my mother talks to me as if I am a confidante. I keep quiet, adopting a thoughtful listening expression. She hesitates before lighting a cigarette. In a low voice, as if the twins might have bugged our kitchen, she says, "For god's sake, never repeat this, but both of them are still virgins. I find that extraordinary."

I too find that extraordinary. "Blimey!" I say, which isn't the required response.

She looks at me, her eyes hard. "I'm warning you. Not a whisper to anyone."

We are not getting on. There is nothing I can do to please my mother. While I am often sullen and resentful, she picks on my every misdemeanour, making a trivial incident into something unforgivable.

I am growing up. Almost overnight, or that is how it seems, I prefer to spend time with friends, I don't want to keep my mother company each evening or go shopping with her at the weekends. I know she dreads the summer without the twins to cheer her up. We both do.

The Thursday before they leave England, as always, they fill our living room with their voices, their perfume, bottles of Martini Bianco, Dry Sack Sherry, cigarettes and, of course, their unquenchable exuberance. Even Lesley, who had seemed reluctant to go away this summer, is excited. The noisier they are, the quieter my mother grows until finally, just before they are due to leave, she bursts into the conversation with a list of my recent wrongdoings: a scarf borrowed and not returned, a wet towel left hanging over the bannisters, failure to tidy my bedroom.

"She treats this house like a hotel, with me here to provide food and money so she can go out with her friends. I should have left her with her father. They deserve each other." Mum turns to me, "How would you have liked that?"

I say, "I'm sorry, Mum."

Her voice is ice cold. "I said, how would you have liked that?"

"I wouldn't have liked it at all." I look at the twins but their eyes – full of sympathy – are on Mum. "Really Mum. I'm sorry. I'll try harder."

She reaches for her ashtray. "What's your apology worth? Sweet FA!"

I'm sitting on the sofa next to Lesley but now I get to my feet. I don't want to argue in front of the twins on their last night with us. They will take my mother's side whether I am in the right or not. Gently I say, "Mum, I really am sorry. I *will* try to be more considerate in future." As I say it, I mean it.

Her face twists into a sneer. "You'll try? How many times have I heard that? Pull the other one, dear – it's got bells on."

Something inside snaps. I am not sorry anymore, I am as angry as she is. I yell at her, "For Christ's sake, how many more times do you want an apology? Get over it!"

Jean's hand lashes out as she slaps my cheek hard. "Don't you dare speak to your mother like that."

My eyes fill with tears of rage. I feel as if I could kill Jean *and* Mum. I put every ounce of hatred into my eyes. Shocked, Mum steps away from me.

Lesley, looking appalled, shrinks back into the corner of the sofa. "Jeanie," she whimpers, "you should never hit a child."

"She's a galumphing young woman now and she deserved it." To me, Jean says, "You're getting too big for your boots."

I go out into the garden. Five minutes later Lesley joins me. She drapes her cardigan around my shoulders.

"You're in the soup now," she says, but with humour.

"I'm always in the soup."

"I know. Try to understand your mother a little – she can't help the way she is. Some women just aren't mother material." Lesley laughs bleakly. "Let's think – if Dot hadn't been your mum, what would she have been?"

My shoulders relax while I think over my answer. I can easily imagine Mum as Marlene Dietrich in a trench coat and beret. "Perhaps a spy."

Lesley nods.

"Seducing information out of powerful, wicked men?"

"There you are then," Lesley says. "Imagine how disappointing it is for her to spend an entire life looking after you and typing letters."

Later, in my bedroom, I think about the slap from Jean. Studying my reflection in the wardrobe mirror, I can find no mark on my cheek. I think how my opinion of Jean hasn't changed. She is dazzling, she is funny, but she has no kindness or understanding... but still I want her to like and admire me.

With the twins away and no one for Mum to share tales of my daily wrongdoings with, she and I begin to get along a little bit better. Lesley's words about Mum's life being a disappointment have had an effect. I see my mother in a different, kinder light.

One sunny Saturday morning we stroll to the nearby shopping centre, making a stop en route to visit Tuson's, Mum's favourite second-hand furniture shop, or 'antique emporium' as she prefers to call it. She has a word with the proprietor, Daphne Matthews, a sturdy woman who favours tweed and dresses in the style of the Queen holidaying at Balmoral.

Mum says, 'Daphne Matthews could sell camel dung to the Egyptians."

She can certainly sell my mother second-hand furniture. This particular Saturday a pair of enormous armchairs are on display outside the shop.

Mum murmurs, "You don't get armchairs like these anymore."

I agree that you don't. We lower ourselves into them. I feel a circular spring pressing against my buttock, but not too insistently.

"They're a darn sight more comfortable than the ones we've got at home," Mum says.

Daphne Matthews is watching us from the shop doorway. "They've been re-covered in a Plumbs exclusive country floral," she calls out.

"And Plumbs is?" Mum asks.

Daphne strolls towards us and strokes the back of one of the armchairs. "*La crème de la crème* in furnishing fabrics."

"*La crème de la crème*," Mum repeats and hauls herself out of the chair. She looks at me. "What do you think?"

"About what?"

"The armchairs of course. Should I buy them?"

"Depends on how much they are."

"Oh, they're very reasonable." Daphne pauses. "Considering their desirability."

It doesn't take us long to realise that Mum's highly desirable armchairs are far too big for our sitting room. They dwarf the sofa and leave no space at all for the coffee table. Within a week the springs in both seats are pressing their way through the exclusive Plumbs fabric and the horse-hair stuffing begins to leak out of the cushions. The window cleaner advises Mum to get the chairs resprung. "Although respringing might cost more than you paid for 'em," he says cheerfully.

Mum is horrified. "But I paid ninety pounds for each chair! Daphne Matthews said they're worth twice that much!"

The window cleaner grins. "Well, Daphne Matthews is a fibber," he says. "I can recommend a good upholsterer." Which is how Arthur comes into our lives.

While away in Italy, the twins send their usual scrawled postcards. "Views fabulous! Having a rip-roaring time!" Then one evening at the end of August, Mum receives a phone call. After a moment she carries the phone into the living room and shuts the door. I am in my bedroom trying out several new hairstyles only possible now that my hair is longer, when she calls up to me, "Can you run to the off licence and buy our usual?"

I don't much like being asked to 'run' anywhere but I am curious. I'm only ever sent to buy 'our usual' on the Thursdays when the twins are in England.

"Who was on the phone?" I ask.

"Jean. She and Lesley are coming over."

"But they're not due back till September."

Mum sighs. "Just do as you're told. Get peanuts and crisps as well."

By the time I return from the off licence, the twins' car is already parked outside our house. Mum meets me at the front door. She takes the carrier bag and holds out her hand. "Change please. They're here."

"I saw the car."

"You can't talk to them tonight."

"Why not?"

"Because I said not. It might be best if you went straight up to your bedroom."

"I never go to bed this early."

Mum gives me a look. "On this occasion you will do as I tell you."

We haven't seen either of the twins since the night of the argument. I have no idea how Jean or I will react to each other. As I head for the stairs, the living room door opens and Jean appears, a little unsteady on her feet.

"Hello sweetheart." She throws her arms around me, planting a kiss on my cheek as if this isn't the same cheek she'd slapped. Her breath smells of wine. "Bless. Going to the shops at this time of night. Next week we'll hear all your news. Lesley's not up to scratch tonight."

Over Jean's shoulder, I catch a glimpse of Lesley, sprawled against the sofa cushions, blonde hair tousled, her pink trouser suit creased as if she's slept in it.

Mum pokes my shoulder blade. "Vamoose!" she says, before steering Jean back into the room and closing the door behind them.

I read for a while and then switch off the lamp. Miraculously, any anger I've harboured for Jean has disappeared. I fall asleep. The sound of their car driving out of our road wakes me. It is twenty past two. Downstairs I hear Mum washing glasses. I fall asleep again.

The following morning, while I'm still in bed, Mum brings me a cup of tea and one for herself, which is unusual. She wears the pretty silk dressing gown that I envy and hope one day she'll pass on to me. Its pastel colours suit her. Mum always looks tired but sometimes, in the mornings if I pay attention, I catch a glimpse of the pretty, hopeful young woman she'd once been. This is to be one of those mornings.

I punch my pillow into shape and put it behind my head. Mum takes her cigarettes and lighter from her pocket and sits down at the foot of the bed.

"The dog's messed on the stairs again," she says quite cheerfully.

"I'll clear it up before I go to school."

"Do it properly."

"Will do."

She inhales, then blows a smoke ring towards the window. Quite calmly, almost as if she's telling me that one of the twins has changed her hair colour, she says, "Lesley has been raped."

"What?"

"On a park bench in Rome."

"By her fiancé?"

She frowns. "Are you trying to be funny?"

"No. I just assumed."

"Do you want to know what happened or just keep on asking fatuous questions?"

The rapist wasn't Italian, he was Swedish. In Rome for a sales convention. The twins met him and his work colleague, a French man called Alexandre, in a restaurant one evening. The two men were seated at a table by the window. They'd watched the twins make their spectacular entrance: identical blonde sisters, tall and dressed alike – one in sky blue, the other rose pink, both with silver chiffon scarves fluttering around their tanned shoulders.

The twins sat down. Lesley studied the menu while

Jean studied the room. By then they were two-thirds of the way through their holiday and had gathered no romantic adventures to take home. Initially Jean's gaze passed over these men at the window table. She dismissed them as 'not our type'. But on her second sweep of the room, she recognised the telltale signs of an interested male: the quick, almost furtive glance – then away – then back again. The body language: shoulders forward and fidgeting as if his chair was uncomfortable.

Resting her elbows on the table, chin balanced on her linked fingers, knowing the perfect contrast her blonde hair and blue eyes made against her skin, Jean presented herself to them while murmuring something inconsequential to her sister.

One of the men, the Swede, called the waiter over and said something in a low voice. The waiter glanced across the room towards the twins' table, before nodding. He appeared respectfully amused. A few minutes later, carrying a tray, a bottle of champagne and two champagne flutes, he approached their table.

Jean touched Lesley's hand. "I think we have admirers."

"I hope not. I just want dinner and an early night."

The waiter placed the tray on their table. Jean smiled, Lesley looked surprised. The waiter leant forward and took Lesley's hand. Quite loudly he said, "For the lady with the sad eyes from the gentleman at the window table."

Of course, Lesley was flattered. If Jean was annoyed by the attention her sister was getting, she didn't show it. Instead she instructed the waiter to ask the men – Alexandre and The Swede – to join them. When the meal ended, The Swede paid for Lesley's dinner while Alexandre paid for Jean's. They were the last diners to leave the restaurant. It was nearly one am but Alexandre insisted the night was young and Jean agreed. Lesley was exhausted, her face drawn and pale, lipstick retreating to the edges of her lips. Gallantly, The Swede offered to walk her back to her hotel no more than a hundred yards away. Alexandre and Jean set off in the opposite direction…

Arthur, the upholsterer, is at least ten years older than Mum. He is deaf in one ear, which Mum incomprehensibly concludes is reassuring in a craftsman. Arthur arrives wearing a shabby, crumpled, tweed suit, which she also finds acceptable for a man in his line of work. Arthur wears a ring (but not a pinky ring), which Mum insists implies understated wealth. She wonders whether two men wearing rings arriving in her life in the space of a few months is significant and she wishes she could discuss this with the twins, but this isn't a good time, what with Lesley being devastated.

Arthur manhandles our armchairs into his small van (Mum observes that this demonstrates surprising physical strength) and returns them a few weeks later looking every inch the desirable country style. Even I am impressed because the chairs are now very comfortable… although still too big to allow room for a coffee table. Few things have ever pleased my mother, but the reupholstering and repair to the armchairs exceed all her expectations.

In Arthur's good ear, Mum remarks, "Arthur, you're a genius."

He gives her a tiny self-deprecating smile, his grey cheeks reddening slightly as he reduces his bill from fifty pounds to ten. He then offers to remove the scratch on Mum's walnut chest of drawers. "I could French polish that for you," he says.

"Could you?"

"No charge. My pleasure."

After he's gone, taking the chest with him, I notice that Mum is singing Petula Clark's 'Downtown' under her breath.

"You don't fancy Arthur, do you?"

"Of course not, but I think he may have a soft spot for me."

"He's old."

"There's many a good tune –"

"Don't!"

"You are a prude."

Arthur brings back an immaculate chest of drawers and takes away the dining table to French polish. By then they are going out together. Mum's lipstick changes from Matt Peach to Scarlet Rose. With Mum's advice, Arthur buys a new suit, several pairs of slacks, shirts, and begins wearing a cricket pullover knotted around his neck. I don't know who to disapprove of the most: Arthur with his apologetic way of entering any room, or Mum emulating a vivacious hummingbird.

Lesley was grateful when The Swede tucked her hand under his arm. She felt comforted and taken care of and apologised for seeming so tired. "I have diabetes. I carry a bar of chocolate with me in case my sugar level drops." She showed him the bar of Cadbury's milk chocolate she kept in her handbag. He seemed to think that she was offering him the chocolate. He took the bar from her and broke off a piece. Snapping this in two, he popped a square into Lesley's mouth and one into his own. Then he dropped the remains of the bar into his jacket pocket. They continued walking towards the hotel, Lesley uneasy at the way he'd appropriated her chocolate. With relief she saw ahead the white facade of the hotel, the smoked glass doors and marble pillars.

"A kiss?" he asked. His English was perfect, with only a slight intonation.

A kiss was the last thing Lesley wanted, but she accepted because, in the past, this was often how an evening in Italy ended.

He led her into a tiny park that she knew well. The sisters had sat there on numerous occasions with Antonios and Marios, drinking cappuccino and planning their days. Not much of a park: encircled by wrought-iron railings, one gate, some grass, a gravel path – the whole area no more than twenty-five yards in diameter. They found a bench. Behind it, a hedge of dense shrubbery hid them from the street.

Lesley was relieved to sit down. She felt exhausted and just a little drunk. She thought how wonderful it would be if The Swede would forgo his kiss and instead gather her up in his arms and carry her the last few steps to the hotel. Then deposit her in the lift, murmur something about a memorable evening as the lift doors close, gently shutting out his face and body.

The Swede turned her head to face him and kissed her. Her lips were acquiescent. His tongue darted in between her teeth. Alarmed, her own timid tongue did its best to repel him. His mouth still pressed against hers, he eased her shoulders back against the arm of the bench so that she was half-lying. Her dress rode up, exposing the tops of her stockings. His body covered hers.

"No," she said, trying to push him away. "Stop!"

He took no notice. His lips nuzzled her neck while his hand slid beneath the silk of her knickers.

She tried once more. "Please, don't do this." Her voice sounded ineffectual and pleading but for a moment he stopped, lifting his head and looking up at her. He smiled. She felt a flicker of hope.

"You know you want this. Don't fight me. Enjoy." With

his gaze still locked into hers, he ripped the front of her dress, pulling the material apart to reveal her breasts in their black lacy bra. "Yum-yum," he said. (When, a few days later, Lesley repeats this to Mum, she is embarrassed, as if she fears The Swede's boyish 'yum-yum' will make my mother feel kindlier towards him.)

Concentrating now, he eased aside her bra straps, cupped one breast in his hand and squeezed.

Lesley felt incapable of fighting back. She fixed her thoughts on her sister – the strong one. Jean would never allow herself to get into such a situation. Any man would think twice before attempting to overpower her.

The Swede pinched her nipple. "Don't fall asleep." His voice was harsh and then he bit into the soft flesh of her breast, drawing blood.

With strength Lesley didn't know she had, she jerked her head back then forwards, smashing her chin down against the crown of The Swede's head.

"Ugh!" His grip loosened, shoulders slumping, as she tried to struggle free.

She didn't see his fist coming, just felt it crack against her cheek bone. She saw stars. All The Swede's now ferocious activity seemed to be happening at a distance. He was forcing his way into her. The pain made her gasp. She had random thoughts: he must be so uncomfortable. Where was his other leg? Her dress would be ruined. What an awful noise he was making: "Ah-ah-ah-aaah."

She stopped struggling. Let him get on with it – and in truth it didn't go on for long. Soon, he was tidying her up; pulling down her dress, covering her breasts and positioning her limbs as if she was a shop mannequin. Satisfied that he'd returned her almost to the state in which he'd started, he offered her another square of chocolate. She shook her head.

"I'm sorry about your face," he said stiffly.

At that she even attempted a painful smile. Again, he tried to force chocolate between her lips but this time she gritted her teeth against him. She felt sick, hypersensitive to the smell of his fingertips behind the smell of chocolate.

And then she was on her own. For half an hour she sat, just waiting. Imagining any attempt to leave the park might bring him back. Finally, fearfully, her chiffon scarf covering her bruised face and her naked shoulders, she returned to the hotel. The rape was never reported to the police. The only people the twins ever told were Mum (who told me) and their friend Eileen. That night, both sisters lost their virginity.

We do not see the twins again for a month, although Mum speaks to them almost daily on the telephone. Because Mum is seeing Arthur, she recounts everything to him now and I am left out.

When on a Thursday in September they finally arrive at our house, it is as if nothing unpleasant has happened during their holiday. They bring gifts: Italian chocolates and earrings for Mum, a beaded shoulder bag for me.

Mum mentions Arthur and his French polishing skills but, before she can elaborate, Jean holds aloft her gin and tonic and shouts, "Darlings, a bit of good news at long last!"

Mum, cut short as she's about to lead them over to admire her newly polished dining table, looks bewildered. "Well, Arthur really isn't much of a conquest," she says.

"Bless her," Jean yells. "Not your Arthur – although we're thrilled, aren't we, Lesley?" Lesley nods but her expression is strained.

Jean sips her drink. "I couldn't mention this before." She

lowers her voice and glances again at her sister. "Because of you know what."

"You're engaged," I say.

Jean's face breaks into a huge smile, her eyes dance. "Clever you! Not quite, but almost! This time it's the real thing. It's Alexandre. The man I met on holiday."

Mum says, "But wasn't he the friend of – ?"

"Only a colleague, never a friend," Jean says.

There will be no fiancé stage, no engagement, just a wedding, and afterwards Jean will move into Alexandre's Paris flat.

After they go, I say to Mum, "That will be difficult for Lesley, won't it? Her sister marrying the friend of the bloke who raped her."

"As Jean says, he was only a colleague."

"Even so –"

"The twins were very stupid to go off alone with strangers. I'd have expected Lesley to have more sense."

"But you do feel sorry for her?"

Mum hesitates. "I don't know."

"But not only has Lesley been raped –"

"Don't repeat that to a soul!"

"She's lost her sister as well. They've never been apart before."

"Can we stick with the romance of the situation?" Mum wants to see Jean's forthcoming marriage as a vindication for patience. The twins have stuck to their guns in their search for a man and at least one of them has struck gold. "Anyway, at thirty-five, the twins are far too old to be virgins."

"Is being a virgin a bad thing?" I ask her.

"Virgins end up withered, yellow faced and sour."

The world according to my mother.

*

Weeks go by. Lesley's rape is forgotten in the excitement over Jean's forthcoming wedding, although no date has been settled on. Alexandre visits the twins at home and meets their family, who declare him a charming man. Now he is taking Jean to stay at his flat for the first time. They are going to choose new curtains and if possible spend some time with *his* family.

Jean is a changed woman, quieter and kinder. I realise how desperate she must have been as the years flew by and she and her sister became a permanent fixture. Jean never wanting to be one half of 'the twins'. She wanted to be Mrs Someone.

"The curtains won't be cheap," Jean tells us the week before the Paris trip. "Whichever fabric we choose, he'll be stuck with it and me for the foreseeable future."

"He'll be stuck with you forever, bless his heart!" Lesley says. "I'm so happy for you, sweetheart."

"We all are." Mum turns to me. "Cathy, do you want a ginger wine?"

"I'd rather have a gin and tonic."

They all laugh. "Oh well, why not?" Mum says.

"Bless her as well!" the twins shout, whether for Mum or me.

Jean goes to Paris, but she and Alexandre spend the days and nights in bed and no curtain-choosing or family visits occur. On her return, Jean tells us she isn't worried because they have the rest of their lives for these tasks. Alexandre's flat is very bare, completely lacking any softer, womanly touches: a double bed in the bedroom, only a leather sofa and a smoked-glass coffee table in the living room, a set of monochrome prints in the hall. While she was there, they did visit a market on Sunday morning for fresh pastries and coffee. From a stall she bought him an Afghan rug in reds and orange to go next to the bed.

"He almost cried," Jean tells us, herself misty-eyed. "No one's ever shown him love before. His ex-wife treated him like shit."

This is the first we've heard of an ex-wife. I am aware of a stillness in Lesley. She sits very straight in one of the big armchairs, her face unreadable, hands clasped in her lap.

Jean looks at Mum. "Lesley doesn't approve of Alexandre having an ex-wife."

"It's only that he'd never mentioned her before," Lesley answers.

"Maybe he thought I'd have the same po-faced reaction as you." Jean's voice is cold.

"Freshen our drinks please, Cathy," Mum says.

Autumn turns into winter. Jean makes two further trips to Paris but no more is said about a wedding. Between the two sisters there is tension. Their visits to us are quieter and more bad-tempered. Small arguments crop up – brief, heated exchanges – a 'you said, she said, he said' type of thing.

It is my eighteenth birthday, a Tuesday. I intend to go out with friends to celebrate in a local pub. While I'm upstairs getting ready, the front doorbell rings. I hear Mum opening the door. "Jean, whatever's the matter?" she says, followed by the sound of someone sobbing. I stand at the top of the stairs and look down into the hall. There is Jean in my mother's arms. She looks up at me and I realise that I've never seen the twins' faces without makeup before. Jean looks dreadful; much older, washed out, distraught.

I telephone my friends and cancel. While Mum comforts

Jean, the two of them squashed into one of the big armchairs, I fix drinks: tea, alcohol and eventually coffees.

Alexandre has been stringing her along. He's put off all discussion of a wedding with lies and excuses: his parents are seriously ill, a brother bankrupt, dissatisfaction with his job. The truth is, Alexandre is still married, still shares a house outside Paris with his wife. In fact, he asserts that he loves his wife and it is the French way to run a wife and a mistress. His flat is just a rented *pied-à-terre*, useful for work. None of this comes out until Jean forces his hand. She is pregnant. She imagines he will be thrilled at her news. So many times, he's told her how much he regrets not having children.

But he does have children: a boy and a girl. They are enough for him. He offers to arrange and pay for an abortion. She refuses.

Jean is broken-hearted. Mum and I have never seen her like this before and the enormity of her sorrow eclipses all our own petty jealousies, annoyances, and hopes for *our* futures.

Mum says the right thing. "If he'd only accepted the baby, you wouldn't have minded that he was married. You'd have been happy to share him, wouldn't you?"

Gratefully, Jean looks up at Mum. "Lesley doesn't understand, but you do, don't you, Dot? If you love someone you'll accept just about any bloody indignity to keep them."

Mum nods. "Don't I know it?" she says.

So, do Lesley and Jean live happily ever after? Well, yes, they do.

Jean has a baby boy, Pauly. By then Lesley has already given *her* heart to the idea of having a nephew or niece to care for. Both sisters love Pauly to bits. Together they buy a house a mile away from their parents and make it into the home they've always wanted for themselves. Lesley continues to work, providing for Jean and the baby. They become a family. I don't believe either woman regrets the way their lives have turned out. With the advent of Pauly, they see less of us, but it is a gradual easing away and, looking back, I think almost a relief on both sides. Mum loved the twins as the adventuresses they once were, but twins accompanied by a crying baby or a spoilt little boy hold no appeal whatsoever.

Arthur is not to be the love of my mother's life. Many years later, I discover that the love of her life came and went while I wasn't paying attention, but that's the stuff of novels. For several years Mum continues to go out with Arthur and during that time every stick of wooden furniture we have is repaired and repolished. When, finally, Mum runs out of jobs for Arthur, the relationship reaches a natural conclusion. However, the positive 'Arthur effect' – that belief that she is still a desirable woman – lasts Mum for a few years more, and by the time it fades forever I am already embarking on my own mistakes.

For the twins and Mum, no matter how much I adore and love them, I remain the child who is of no real importance, who makes the drinks and fills up the crisp bowl – the child to be sent off to bed while the grown-ups talk. Perhaps that is only fair and right, because this story is primarily about them – not me.

II

Father & Daughter

"There's a beech hedge," I told the cab driver.

He nodded. "We're not there yet."

The road meandered on through fields. I picked out the odd roof of a farm building but no sign of any real habitation. The cab turned right onto what appeared to be a bridleway, but after twenty yards, the path widened and became an uneven road running between two grassy banks. On each side, I saw the dirty white woollen legs of sheep, a head lowered to graze. I had the unnerving sensation of travelling downwards to an underground destination, and then with a jolt we swung out into a road of large detached houses and I sensed my father's presence. Somewhere nearby – behind hedge, tree, pebbledash frontage – he was waiting, pacing an airy bedroom, changing and rechanging his clothes.

"This is it."

The taxi mounted a grass verge. I'd remembered a hedge of glossy leaves but the hedge still wore the dead brown leaves of the previous autumn. It was ten minutes past eleven.

"Don't come any earlier than eleven," he'd said in his last letter. "Because I won't be ready. I don't like being rushed in the morning. But not too late either. You know me..."

Yes, I did.

"So, I'll collect you around four?" the driver was saying.

"Exactly four pm."

He smiled. "Don't worry. Ray Baker's an old customer. I know his ways."

I glanced at my watch. Time was ticking by. "How much do I owe you?" I opened my purse.

"Mr Baker's settled up."

"Thank you," I said. "I'll see you later."

"You will."

In the years following my last visit there had been changes. The walls, which had surely been a pale cream limestone, were now covered in ivy, cut back around the windows. The house resembled one woven into a tapestry – each green ivy leaf an individual stitch. Under the two bay windows stood stone urns filled with spring flowers. There were signs that someone had been raking the gravel drive.

The porch door was unlocked. I stepped in. The interior was lined with racks of plate-glass shelving crammed with plastic flower-pots of over-wintering pelargoniums. They gave off a peculiarly hot tropical smell. I registered a mild dismay. Not for one moment could I imagine my father bothering to over-winter plants. I felt something like affection for him, mixed with my usual apprehension, knowing he would be standing on the other side of the door waiting for me to ring the brass doorbell. He would have seen the taxi arrive, wondered what it was I said to the driver and he to me, watched as I walked towards the house, attempting to read the expression on my face. I pressed the bell.

The door flew open. In a silence that lasted no more than a few seconds we assessed each other.

He wore an olive-green short-sleeved shirt and tan trousers. I noted his heavy gold watch and then with surprise realised that he was wearing carpet slippers.

"Hello Cath, got a kiss for your old dad?" He made an awkward boyish movement of his body that big men are prone to make to disguise uncertainty. I forced myself to look into his face. He didn't look a day older. His eyes were the same grey-blue as mine, same wide forehead, same dark blonde hair. To kiss his cheek, I had to stretch up. I'm tall but he was taller.

He looked delighted to see me. "Come on in then. Mind the rug."

Like the over-wintering plants, the rug also struck an unfamiliar note. It was a leopard skin. An Indian leopard, he later told me – bought at auction.

"There's a story attached to that but I won't upset your finer feelings."

It sprawled across the beige fitted carpet, head raised, gaping jaws, glass eyes staring furiously into an open-plan sitting room. Gingerly, I stepped over the head and followed.

"I saw you clocking the slippers. Trouble with my metacarpals."

We sat on leather chesterfields facing each other. He'd split up a nest of small tables to accommodate my gin and tonic and bowl of peanuts. It was eleven fifteen am.

"Nothing to be done," he was saying. "Poor circulation. No big deal. I was never much of a walker. I've everything I want here and the wherewithal to keep it looking immaculate." He waved a hand to signify the house's general immaculate state.

"The gravel drive was certainly immaculate," I said. *Now why had I said that and why accept a gin and tonic at this early hour?*

Father & Daughter

As he'd carried the cut-glass tumbler in from the kitchen, he'd said, "I won't join you. I need a clear head to prepare the lunch." He'd sat down again, hands on his knees. I could see the effort he was making. He had changed. He'd lost confidence and was trying to hide it.

"And do you ever see anyone from the factory?" I asked, as if I really was desperate to know. "Your secretary? Your driver, Eric?"

Dad slumped back against the cushions, staring at me as if he considered such a question extraordinary.

"Only you used to get on really well with your staff..." I trailed away.

Now he looked bewildered. Although I knew this to be an act, it still affected me in the same way – that sense of being forced to climb up a down escalator.

He glanced out of the window as if gathering thoughts that I in my appalling ignorance had scattered, before turning back and saying emphatically, "My dear, I got on with my staff because that's the only way to run a business." He rapped his knuckles on the arm of the sofa. "They meant nothing to me. Less than nothing – past, water under the bridge, *finito*." His expression softened. "My secretary, Marge Stocking, gets a good pension out of the firm. Eric and his wife moved to Ramsgate. Every Christmas they send cards – I don't reciprocate. Your hair looks nice. What products do you use?"

"Different brands."

"I suppose you can get away with that, when you're young. Your hair's still resilient. I'm glad you decided to grow it again. Not a bad cut. London salon? What do you think of my conservatory?"

As ever, his lightning change of topic unnerved me. I twisted my head to look at the conservatory opening out from the far end of the room. It was a frieze of hard, bright colour: geraniums, fuchsia, bougainvillea.

"And what about my bougainvillea?" He pronounced it boo-gan-vill-yar. He made the word somehow erotically suggestive. He could manage the same trick with 'apparatus', 'taramasalata', 'sophistication'. I was never quite sure whether this was purely an accident or one of his tricks.

"It's doing admirably," I said.

"Admirably?" he raised an eyebrow. "How's your mother, the sainted Dorothy?"

He took me for what he called 'The Grand Tour'. Upstairs, opening on to a light-filled landing that was bigger than my whole flat at home, were four bedrooms. On a marble-topped table stood a vase of silk hydrangeas, with more silk flowers on the wide windowsills.

"And this is my room," he said finally. I hesitated in the doorway, letting him rush inside and turn to face me, his expression pleased. "I've just had it decorated. Come on in. Don't be shy."

I took two steps into the room. He was already over by the window looking out. "You can just about see the church from up here. When there's a storm I watch it raging around the valley like a trapped animal." He looked back at me. "You can't see anything from over there."

"Yes, I can. It's a beautiful room."

"Best room in the house. The wardrobe's flame mahogany. Cost a fortune." He opened one of the windows. "Come and look at this."

Reluctantly, I crossed the room.

"That cypress tree at the bottom of the garden. Did I point it out the last time?"

I shook my head. The last time I'd come with my brother. There had been no gin and tonics, no lunch, no Grand Tour.

"I call him the Sentinel. He keeps guard over my property."

Again, he looked so pleased with himself. He wanted to show off his treasures and have me admire them. He'd settle happily for pretence – that I thought him a great fellow.

I said, "You seem to have been converted to nature."

He grinned at me. "That's one way of putting it, but yes. All happened a bit too late in life. Do you have a garden at home?"

"A small one."

"And do you love it?"

"I do like gardening."

He looked at me – that clear gaze of his when I had no idea what was running through his mind.

We went back downstairs. He left me with a fresh gin and tonic while he went into the kitchen to prepare our lunch.

I poured two-thirds of my drink into a pot of maidenhair fern, starting as he called from the kitchen, "Take your glass and sit at the dining table. There's a cracking view of the garden. At this time of year, with the bulbs and spring flowers, it's gorgeous."

It *was* gorgeous. An old, York stone terrace led to a lawn and circular rose bed. No roses yet, but masses of daffodils and crocus and winter pansies. And a bird table.

Behind my chair, I followed his movements on the other side of a pair of white louvre doors: opening cupboards, his slippered steps shuffling over to the sink, back to the fridge-freezer. At one point, he appeared out in the garden, right in front of the window, heading across the terrace with a tea towel over one arm and carrying a plate full of breadcrumbs. Some he scraped onto the bird table, the rest he tossed on the lawn.

I knew that he knew I would be watching him. That he'd be chuckling to himself at my surprise: *Dad feeding the birds, Dad acting out of character.* I could tell he was exhilarated yet anxious. He wanted my approval, for me to find him lovable. And yes, the sight of my father out there feeding birds, the vulnerability of the unfamiliar ill-fitting carpet slippers, did affect me. That dreaded softening of my heart.

"Grab the Chablis." He burst through the louvre doors, carrying two steaming dinner plates, the wine tucked under his arm.

I eased the bottle away from him. "Should I open it?"

"Yes, yes. Corkscrew on sideboard."

He set the plates on National Trust table mats and rushed back into the kitchen. "Wait for the hollandaise!" he bellowed.

I heard the sound of frantic saucepan stirring.

"Not bad for a bloke on his own," he said, sitting down at the table. He shook out his napkin. "Salmon steaks, the easiest thing in the world. Tinned Norfolk Royal potatoes, frozen peas and Dad's special recipe hollandaise sauce. Get stuck in."

He leant across the table and poured the Chablis. "Well, cheers!" He was almost shouting.

"Cheers," I said.

As he ate, he began to smile. He was about to speak and savouring the pause first. He wiped his chin with his napkin, tossing it onto his side plate, opened his mouth, closed it before taking up his knife and fork again. "I wanted to tell you how pleased I am to see you. It's been a long time. Too long – and I'm not referring to that unfortunate visit with your brother. He wasn't invited and you shouldn't have brought him along – end of story. Now *our* rift, whatever it might have been, and please spare me any details, but I take full responsibility. I deeply regret, regretted at the time, all in the distant past..."

I thought I recognised discomfort, embarrassment, even shame in his eyes, but I was mistaken.

"But you remain my daughter." He coughed out the words as if they'd been blocking his throat. His head swung towards me, searching for some response.

"I do," I said.

That seemed to satisfy him. He relaxed and began to talk. My father was a good, seductive talker. As he'd always done, he asked me questions. He recalled my answers to questions he'd asked me years ago.

I wanted to ask my own question, but he gave me no chance. At one point, I almost found my voice.

He was savouring his Chablis, eying the wine with happy complacency.

I reached for my glass. I was about to ask, "Why?" But then I realised that one word wouldn't be enough. More words would splurge out of me. As I hesitated, he intercepted my hand and squeezed it.

"I'll fetch the pud," he said. "Stack the plates and leave them at the end of the table. I'll fill the dishwasher later."

Back in the kitchen I heard him opening two tins. I knew one would be custard, the other fruit. Custard into saucepan, the hiss of a gas jet.

With the tinned apricots and custard, we drank a red burgundy. I recounted family stories about aunts, uncles and cousins, knowing how much he enjoyed hearing about all these diverse characters linked by blood or emotional ties. I told him Mum had followed her sister Kit to the south coast.

He frowned. "You do know your aunt's a lesbian?"

"Yes," I said.

"And how about you? Any boyfriends? Girlfriends?"

I didn't answer.

"I can't really imagine you turning gay!" His frown turned to an inward smirk.

"Dad, don't think you're safe," I said, finally finding some courage.

Spoon in air, he stopped, "What?"

"You're not safe."

He put down the spoon and began stroking his jaw, trying to become the image of a wise father in reflective mood. "I choose to think I *am* safe." And then, "I believe the housekeeper's left a selection of cheeses somewhere in the kitchen."

"I can't manage any more food."

"You may change your mind. Fish the claret glasses out of the sideboard."

From the kitchen, he emerged triumphantly, carrying a plate of cheeses adorned with dark purple grapes. "Come on. You'll take a drop of claret with your old dad?"

"No thanks."

"Just a sip. Tell me what you think of it. You used to scream blue murder to sip from my glass when you were a little girl."

Just the memory of me as a little girl screaming blue murder for a sip from his glass made me feel cold inside. I couldn't bear the tension – the him against me – me against him. I couldn't bear to disappoint his expectations of the day either. Hemmed in by crystal glassware, I gulped a mouthful of claret. What next? *A fine liqueur, my darling daughter?*

"It's delicious."

"Delicious?"

Then, as if some tension had finally left his body, he

slumped slightly in his chair. When he next began to talk, his voice was quieter, more considering. He told me about a squirrel and a family of magpies who lived in the Sentinel, who terrorised the bird table.

"They're my enemies. I wage war on them. They chase the smaller birds off the table. I don't find squirrels sweet, you know, they're bloody vermin."

He told me about the elderly couple on the left-hand side who kept chickens; brown Leghorns. How every afternoon, the chickens marched into his garden, "Like a line-up from *The Magnificent Seven*. Ok pardner, we're running you out of town."

He told me about his neighbour on the right-hand side who owned the funeral parlour down in the village and parked the hearse out on the drive every night. "Can't be bothered to manoeuvre it into the garage."

He was growing a little drunk. We both were. Outside, the afternoon was drawing in. We sat forward in our chairs, elbows resting on the table.

"Not that I have anything to do with these people. I don't speak to them any more than I have to, which is very little. It's what I glean through conversations overheard and actions witnessed. Do you ever do that?"

"Sometimes."

"I can make up the lives I want. In my head, funeral chappie drinks himself into oblivion every night and couldn't get it up to save his life. It's all in here." He banged his forehead with the heel of his hand. "I don't need any true facts."

I couldn't say my time with my father was a complete misery. There were moments when I realised I was almost enjoying his company. In some underlying way, our years apart had made little difference. I watched and listened, knowing he was trying to charm me, so that later, if I thought back over the past, I would see how he was now to be the truth, and the other man a fiction.

At four o'clock exactly, he lifted the net curtain and there was the same taxi waiting in the driveway.

"You'll be okay?" he said.

"Yes. I'm getting the six fifteen train back into London. Should be home by eight."

"Good."

Slightly unsteadily, I followed him into the hall. We both stepped over the leopard's head. At the front door, we faced each other.

"I'll be in touch," he said. "Give your old dad a kiss."

I hesitated, then tried to peck his cheek.

"Not like that," he said. He pressed his mouth against my lips. I felt the quick rasp of his tongue on mine.

I jerked my head away.

Dad opened the door and the late afternoon sunlight streamed into the hall. Half-blinded, I stumbled across the gravel.

"Ring when you get home," Dad called after me.

Ignoring him, I climbed into the cab. As the car pulled out of the drive, I wiped my mouth with my sleeve. I wanted my father to die, chiefly for my own sake, but also for my brother. We needed the handprints he'd left across our lives to fade.

III

The Lovely Nieces

Kit was my mother's sister. As far as I was concerned she was never an aunt; always a woman I loved and admired, yet couldn't quite manage to feel at ease with. I did think that if there was a god, the god would have been Kit-like, and I would retain my place in her head and her heart – not the most beloved person, but still of value.

Tentatively, on tiptoe like a thief, although this flat is now mine, I enter her bedroom. On the table next to the double bed stands a framed photograph. For as long as I can remember I've been aware of the photograph belonging in this room; Kit moving it from bedside table to mantelpiece to dressing table and back. Once, I found the photograph lying face down on the window seat cushions. It remained there for several days before being returned to the bedside table.

It is a sepia picture of an Edwardian man and woman sitting outside on a bench in front of a window. The frame – which I covet – is art nouveau and made of soapstone, a material that resembles ivory. This I intend to keep. I'll leave the photograph in the carrier bag with other memorabilia from Kit's life, for the family to trawl through after the funeral.

I remove the hardboard backing and the photograph

flutters down onto the carpet. I concentrate on wiping away the accumulated dust on both sides of the rectangle of glass with one of Kit's beautifully laundered, masculine handkerchiefs. Replacing the glass and board, I hold the frame away from me, smiling with pleasure at the thought of owning such a fine thing. But then I'm aware of the vague sense of shame I so often experience around my family, because every family member, both deceased and living, seems to be more vibrant and capable of love than I'll ever be.

Retrieving the photograph, I briefly glance at the couple. Maybe a hundred years ago, a photographer lowered his head under the dark cloth covering his camera. "Smile please," he called out. In one hand he held a flash. It made a small explosive sound and the couple for a moment were dazzled.

I was worried that Kit would swallow her dentures. All those years of her flashing a perfect smile and I'd never known her teeth were false. I wondered if my cousin Paula knew. Each time our paths crossed during visiting hour, I intended to ask, but part of me thought this was a crass subject to discuss when Kit was so ill.

Kit never married, never had children of her own. Instead she had nieces: me, Paula, Hazel and Noreen. There *were* other nieces but they lived some distance away and never got to know her as we did. Up till quite recently Kit was still describing us as her 'lovely, glamorous nieces', although the four of us were in our forties and fifties and hadn't been lovely or glamorous for years. She had nephews as well but they counted for little.

I am the youngest. Because of this and the exotic presents she brought back for me from her travels abroad, up till the age of eighteen I assumed myself to be her favourite. However, talking to my cousins over the last few days, I've realised that at one time or another all of us imagined ourselves to be her favourite.

When I was five years old, Kit gave me a doll. I was in bed and almost asleep. Mum switched on my bedside lamp. "Wake up, Cathy, your aunt has a present for you."

A young woman who looked like a young man stood in the doorway. She was taller than Mum with blue-black hair – a curl at the front drooping down onto her forehead like Elvis Presley. She wore a checked lumberjack style of shirt and slacks, which was unusual – in those days women rarely wore trousers. She strode across the room and leant over my bed. There were fine lines around her eyes and mouth, her skin was lightly tanned, whereas my mother was pale even in summer. The next day Mum explained that Kit had lived abroad since before I was born, working as a journalist. She'd recently bought a flat near the town centre, which she would use when in England. Mum didn't call it a flat, she called it 'a bolt hole'. Mum never approved of Kit, she may not even have liked her – I could tell this from the tone of voice she used when talking about her sister.

Kit set the doll down next to the lamp. The doll's curly hair became a golden halo. "Her name is Lydia," Kit said firmly.

Mum said, "That's a very grown-up name for a child's doll."

Kit grinned at her. Mum looked away.

The doll measured about ten inches from the top of her head down to crocheted bootees. Lydia was not a fashionable doll. Nobody would envy me owning her, but she was very pretty, with bright blue eyes and scarlet lips slightly parted to reveal two tiny teeth. Her dress was leaf green.

At school there were girls who had dolls almost as tall as

they were, but *I* preferred small dolls. Even tiny ones. I had a baby doll from a Christmas cracker that slept in half a walnut shell. Her bedding was a piece of cotton wool from Mum's makeup bag. I owned other dolls – three and four inches tall – bought from Woolworths with my pocket money. Until the arrival of Lydia, my one exception to a maximum height requirement was Teenage Doll. I don't know where she came from. She wore plastic underwear and plastic high-heeled sandals.

The dolls (except for Lydia) lived inside a toy garage my brother didn't play with anymore. The garage had metal petrol pumps and an exterior car lift. Teenage Doll enjoyed herding the little dolls onto the lift floor, winching the lift up to the height of the garage's flat roof and then letting it slam down to the ground, sending the dolls flying.

My brother's name is Steven. Dad (who lived far away in the Midlands) sent Steven to boarding school on the Isle of Wight when I was ten and Steven eleven. Dad said my brother needed a masculine environment. Kit agreed. She said all males over the age of five should be shipped off to a distant island and forgotten about. She pretended not to remember the names of any of her nephews, referring to Steven as 'the boy' or 'that boy', which made me think of Pip and Miss Havisham from *Great Expectations*. Kit was nothing like Miss Havisham in any other way. She would never have cut herself off from the outside world just because a man left her on her wedding day. She'd have been relieved.

Steven collected battalions of soldiers, sailors, cowboys and Roman centurions. He also had toy tanks, army lorries, and Bren guns that fired matchsticks. When my brother was younger, before he went away, he thought it uproariously

The Lovely Nieces

funny to aim the guns at Teenage Doll's bosoms. Actually, we both thought it was funny. Teenage Doll could look after herself. She *always* retaliated. She was a plastic Amazon. She used the smaller dolls for ammunition, hurling them at his battalions. She kept back the tiny baby and the half walnut shell to use only as a last resort, because if Steven was in a sneaky mood his troops would kidnap the baby and the shell and hold them to ransom. As children, Teenage Doll was very real to us.

Lydia never took part in the skirmishes. She leant against the skirting board, legs stretched out in front of her, and watched. Sometimes she held a tea party with her plastic tea set. All the other dolls sat or (if they didn't have jointed legs) lay around while my brother advanced his marines or cowboys, showering us with matches. Sometimes he'd drive his lorries through the tea party.

I hung on to Lydia, although the bloom had left her cheeks and she had very little hair. I didn't keep her on display, she lay quite comfortably at the back of my underwear drawer.

Once, when I was in my early twenties and about to move into my first flat, Kit came over to help me to pack. By then, I'd decided I was far too old for dolls. Lydia lay face down on my bed waiting to be consigned to the box destined for a charity shop.

"So, you kept my dolly?" Kit sounded so pleased, I immediately decided to hang on to her for at least a few more months.

"Who was the original Lydia?" I'd asked lightly.

Kit, standing over an open packing case, grew still; her eyelids almost hid her eyes. I remember thinking, *she's making up a lie*.

She blinked. Her eyes had reddened, as eyes do when tears

are being held back. She said carefully, "Lydia was the love of my life."

Whether this was true or false, I believed her. "Do you still see Lydia?"

She grinned at me. "That is for me to know and you not to find out."

The day after Kit's seventy-fifth birthday, she took a cab to Worthing Hospital. I didn't know about this till Paula texted me. "Kit in hospital. No need to worry. She should be okay by the weekend."

I didn't worry. I have a busy life of my own these days and aunts and cousins have to take a back seat.

Another text arrived from Paula. "Kit having tests. We're all visiting. Can you?"

Worthing Hospital is only a few miles away from where Paula lives, whereas I'm based in North London. If Kit was seriously ill or on the point of death, I would have dropped everything, but just 'having tests' didn't seem sufficient reason to make the journey. It took ten days and phone calls from both cousins for me to arrive in the hospital ward, only to find Kit sitting up in bed, her now silver hair beautifully styled, head bent over a battered Jules Verne novel.

"Hello Kit." I kissed her cheek.

"Darling," she said, turning her book face-down on the blanket. "I thought you'd forgotten me."

"Pressure of work." An oxygen mask lay on a table next to a jug of water and a plastic cup. "What's that for?"

"No breath." She thumped her chest.

On the other side of the bed stood a navy-blue oxygen tank. I was appalled – in a way, angry with her. I just didn't have the time or patience for someone I cared about to be ill.

The Lovely Nieces

As selfish as it sounds, I will use the word 'inconvenient'.

"I look awful, don't I?" Kit reached for my hand.

"You're a picture of health," I said. "Your hair looks lovely."

"Far too feminine." Kit wrinkled her nose. "Once you're over seventy, hairdressers assume that one style suits all."

The flat, although shabby, is dearly familiar. There are memories of good times spent with Kit, with the cousins. There is a sitting room, bedroom, a study, bathroom and kitchen. A small conservatory leads out onto a patio garden. The study shelves are full of books and mementos that Kit has brought back from her travels. I hear my mother's voice proclaiming, "Dust traps! Get rid of the lot!"

I find a box of tiny glass figurines. Each Christmas I remember Kit hanging them on the tree. She always bought a six-footer, carrying it home with the topmost branches sticking out from the boot of her car. None of us were ever allowed to see the tree till Christmas Eve – and then it was a revelation, magical, the room lit only by white fairy lights, the glass figurines gleaming.

We rarely saw Kit's friends. She kept family and friends apart. Only at Christmas and on her birthday, I'd appreciate how loved she was, the dozens of cards, the phone calls.

Mum was rarely kind about her sister. "She has no choice but to rely on her so-called friends," she'd say. My mother and father – such a strange pair. They considered themselves somehow safe just because once upon a time they'd married and had two children to prove how normal they were. And I suppose they were safe and Kit was not, as I finally realised.

At school I was always the first with my hand up to answer a question, "Miss, miss! Me, miss!"

There was one particular teacher I admired, Miss Bryant. She was small, pale faced and rarely smiled, but when she looked at me, I interpreted the expression in her eyes to be one of fondness. Only later, grown up and thinking back over my school days, I realised the emotion I'd seen in Miss Bryant's eyes had been pity – because without fail, I always came up with the wrong answer. Sometimes, when Miss Bryant shook her head and said, "I'm afraid not, Cathy," I was stunned, certain that a mistake had been made.

I was equally convinced that I would shine in my end-of-year school reports, and yet each year, out of thirty-three pupils in my class, I came thirty-third. On just one memorable occasion, I reached the giddy height of twenty-ninth and rushed round to Kit's flat to share my good news. She was in the kitchen washing up, but immediately wiped her hands dry on a tea towel and hugged me. With the sides of our faces pressed together we stared through the open kitchen window, into a middle distance behind the bird bath, as if we clearly saw a future for me of improving results.

"Winston Churchill was fourteen before he began to shine," Kit said.

Our optimism lasted till the end of the following year, when I returned to my old position at the bottom of the class. Kit stopped citing Winston Churchill but continued with the hugging and middle-distance staring. Once she did say, "So what? I was only good at tennis and PE."

I was with Kit the afternoon she was moved to Shoreham Hospital. The ambulance men were gentle with her. "Don't worry," one of them said. "We've seen it all." Which in no way reassured her.

When her hospital gown rode up at the back as they

shifted her from the bed onto a trolley, Kit was distraught. I wasn't much help. I'm not like my cousins. I've had no kids to bring up, partners to make a fuss of, no grandchildren to dote on. Both Paula and Noreen are brilliant at all the touchy-feely stuff – massaging Kit's hands and feet, combing her hair, moisturising her skin – while encouraging her with compliments and kisses. That afternoon I fumbled awkwardly with Kit's gown, unintentionally drawing attention to her distress rather than diminishing it. As they wheeled the trolley down the corridor, I kept a vapid smile on my face as if we were all embarking on a pleasant outing. In the lift I did hold her hand, hanging on to it through the double doors and out into the ambulance bay. Just for a moment she cheered up, her natural curiosity reasserting itself at the change of scenery.

"It's summer." She was smiling up at the leafy trees with a sort of youthful wonder.

"Still early. Only July," I said.

She frowned. "But who's deadheading my roses?"

"Paula, I expect, or her sisters. You can ask them later."

"Remind me when we see them. You'll come with me in the ambulance?"

"Kit, I can't." In truth I didn't want to.

She looked straight into my eyes and with a sense of shock I thought, "Kit knows exactly what I'm doing or not doing."

I waved as they closed the ambulance doors. "I'll visit in the next few days. Promise." Then, with relief, I walked back through the hospital, through the main entrance and out into the car park.

By the time Kit reached her fifties, she'd moved on from writing articles to becoming a highly respected travel writer. Whichever country she visited, she returned bearing gifts: turquoise beaded sandals from India, scarlet silk pyjamas patterned with dragons from Hong Kong, a suede shoulder bag with my name monogrammed on the clasp from Texas. Dazzling gifts, but as I grew older I began to study them more closely and compare each one against those Kit gave my cousins. Beaded sandals weren't as splendid as saris embroidered with silver and gold thread for Paula and her sisters, pyjamas weren't as exciting as sets of leather luggage, a suede shoulder bag wasn't nearly as stylish as calf-skin cowboy boots with Cuban heels. When Noreen was eighteen, Kit took her to New York. When Paula was eighteen they spent a week in Hawaii. When Hazel was eighteen, Kit paid for her honeymoon in Benidorm.

And then I was eighteen and Kit was going to Paris for five days. Once again, I was certain I had the right answer, of course this time Kit would take *me* with her. I was so excited, I told my friends. On my last day at school, leaving with two dismal A levels, I told my teachers. My friends were envious, the teachers wished me luck. *"Bonnes vacances!"* from the French teacher – a subject in which I failed spectacularly.

Of course, Mum was observing my high spirits just as Miss Bryant had done – with pity. Finally, with only a week to go before Kit's trip, Mum said, "Don't build your hopes up – you don't have a passport."

I knew nothing of passports. I'd never been abroad before. "Do I need one?"

"Of course you do."

"Then we'd better get one."

"There's no point." She laid her hand on my shoulder, which was as near to showing emotion as my mother could manage. "Paula's going with her."

"But it's my turn."

"I'm afraid that 'turns' don't come into it."

"Is it because *you* don't want me to go?"

"It's nothing to do with me," Mum said sharply, her cheeks reddening with anger. "Surely you've noticed how your precious aunt always makes more of a fuss of your cousins."

"Does she?"

I took this painful information up to my bedroom. At any age, finding out that you aren't similarly loved, when you thought you were, is upsetting; at eighteen and lacking confidence, I felt my world was falling apart. But I said nothing and waited, ready to be convinced that Mum was wrong.

Kit went to Paris with Paula. She rang Mum from the hotel and even put Paula on the phone. "Paula wants a word with Cathy," she said.

Mum looked at me. I shook my head. "I'm afraid Cathy's out with some friends from school."

I left Mum to Kit's phone call and went up to my room.

On her return, Kit called in to see us. She came out into the garden to find me. "Hello munchkin," she said cheerfully. "Being good?"

"Of course." I wanted to hate her, but I couldn't help smiling with pleasure just seeing her. In middle age, she still looked the same, with her easy way of strolling rather than walking, jeans now and tee-shirts, a cotton jacket thrown over her shoulders.

Mum followed her out.

"Does munchkin deserve a present?" Kit asked.

"Oh, I think so."

From her shoulder bag Kit took out a small parcel wrapped in gold tissue paper and tied with ribbon. "Close your eyes and open your hands," she said.

I closed my eyes. The tissue paper made a slight crackling

sound; whatever she'd bought me felt incredibly light. I was aware of Kit undoing the ribbon.

"Okay. Open your eyes."

Folded in my hands lay a silk scarf.

"Don't lose it. Hermes. Cost a small fortune."

The scarf was horrible. Horrible colours: red, white and navy, in each corner the image of a Union Jack. Not French at all, more like a souvenir of London. I let the silk slip between my fingers.

Kit caught it. "Hey, I said that cost a small fortune."

My voice was quite cool as if I was speaking to a stranger. "Are you sure someone didn't buy the scarf for *you*, Kit?"

Mum gasped and looked horrified. Kit frowned. "You're being impertinent."

Those three words struck me like an icy shower. My eyes filled with tears.

"I'm sure Cathy didn't intend to be impertinent," Mum said. "But really Kit, a scarf like this is more suited to an older woman."

Kit held up her hands. "Don't shoot the messenger. Paula chose it."

Mum saw the hurt in my face, that Kit hadn't even picked the scarf out for me. "Kit," she said, "sometimes I despair of you."

Their eyes locked.

I was excluded.

Kit looked away first and took a deep breath before turning to me, her face once more full of affection. "I'll have to find something else for you. We could go shopping together. You'd like that."

I shook my head. "There's nothing I really need."

*

The Lovely Nieces

From the floor I retrieve the photograph. I realise I have been uneasy ever since I dismantled the soapstone frame, as if, in my usual careless fashion, I'd ignored something of importance. I make myself a coffee and carry mug and photograph out into Kit's conservatory.

"Take your time," I tell myself, because I never take time over anything.

I rest the photograph against the empty fruit bowl. My assumption is that I shall be studying an image of long dead relatives. I've never been interested in ancestors. I leave it to my cousins to reminisce and compile family trees. I possess no photograph album charting each stage of my life. Under normal circumstances I would have no more than a passing interest in looking at an image of great-grandparents. Dead, buried, gone. Nothing to do with me. But these are not normal circumstances.

The woman's hair is caught up above her head into a tousle of light-coloured curls. She wears elbow-length gloves of black satin and a long dress of a material like bombazine. It has a dull shine. The woman looks as if she's about to laugh or has paused in the middle of laughter. I return to the Edwardian gentleman, who seems stern and unamused... and yet, his eyes – I recognise those eyes.

We were several weeks further along and Kit's false teeth were now consigned to a plastic box in her toilet bag. It had all been quite tragic. Initially, on arriving at Shoreham Hospital, her health improved dramatically. I visited on a Friday afternoon and found my aunt waiting for me in the patients' lounge wearing a pair of navy trousers and a candy-striped shirt. She looked up at me – expression triumphant! "I get out of jail tomorrow," she said.

I sat quietly, letting her talk. I welcomed the return of the old enthusiastic Kit. She recounted her plans: a party to celebrate, a trip abroad in the autumn. "Perhaps you'd come with me," she said. "My treat."

"Let's get you well before we talk about trips abroad." I did manage to stroke her hands as my cousins would have done. Those hands were still tanned and young looking. Expressive hands. I knew them so well, the band of white on her third finger where a familiar ring used to be. Paula had returned it to Kit's flat when she was first admitted to hospital.

At the end of the hour, I walked Kit back to the ward. Unobserved, I stood in the doorway watching her. I sort of drank my aunt in. Her suitcase lay open on the bed and she was folding her pyjamas. I loved her very much. On the train home I made resolutions to visit more regularly, to be a more caring person, to value someone I might not have in my life for much longer.

The next morning Paula telephoned. While putting the last things back into her suitcase, Kit had fallen and fractured her hip.

"She looks terrible," Paula said.

"But I only saw her yesterday and she was fine. Hips mend, don't they?"

Paula sighed. "Would it be too much to ask for you to come down again? You can stay with me."

"For how long?" I didn't want to go back or stay with Paula. All my good intentions evaporated.

"As long as it takes."

"You're being dramatic. Surely Kit can't go from being well enough to be discharged to dying overnight."

My cousin had never raised her voice to me before but now she shouted, "Will you just get your arse down here, you selfish bitch?"

The Lovely Nieces

I got my arse down there. If any one of my relations was capable of intimidating me, it was Paula. I found my way to the ward I'd visited only twenty-four hours earlier. There was no sign of Kit. I hurried back to the nurses' station. "My aunt's not here. Kit Fulbrough?"

"Of course she is. Follow me."

She led me to a bed nearest to the window. A stranger lay propped up on pillows. Over her legs lay just a sheet.

"Kit, you've got a visitor," the nurse shouted as if the woman was deaf. To me she said, "She's been poorly since her fall yesterday. She broke her spectacles but we've stuck them together with Sellotape for now."

The woman lying in the bed looked years older than Kit, her features caved in like a building once the foundations have given way, eyes glittering slits under wine-coloured lids.

"But this is not my aunt," I insisted.

The nurse laughed as if I was being foolish. "Kit," she squeezed the woman's arm. "Another of your nieces. Aren't you a lucky girl?"

Kit was now almost completely withdrawn. Only occasionally – like the shutter of an old-fashioned camera clicking open – there was a faint look of comprehension in her eyes. Once she pulled a face at me. A sort of 'what can I do? I'm stuck with this bloody dying business' face.

Sitting by her bed, I constantly returned to the question that had niggled me for so many years: Kit had loved us all but she'd loved my cousins more – hadn't she?

I arranged to meet Paula one afternoon in Costa Coffee. I don't think she knew what to expect, although from me she probably feared some difficulty. Settled with our coffees, I immediately put the question to her: "Paula, why did Kit favour the three of you over me?"

She had recently given up smoking. Automatically her hands moved to her jacket pockets as if searching for the comfort of a cigarette packet and lighter. Tersely she said, "Kit didn't."

"The gifts, the holidays. The three of you share a closeness with Kit that I'm shut out of."

She coughed a sort of bitter laugh. "You have your father to thank for that."

I was stunned. "Dad lived on the other side of the country. We had virtually no contact with him."

"And yet he arranged for your brother, his ex-wife's favourite child, to be packed off to boarding school as far away as possible from her, on the Isle of Wight." She stirred her coffee vigorously. "Kit offered to take you abroad several times. Your mum always said no. He'd have stopped her alimony. He might even have applied for custody."

"But why?"

"The hypocrisy of a sexual predator? You told me yourself that your dad had a vivid imagination. Kit is gay."

I felt sick inside. I was aware of other customers watching us, straining to hear our conversation. "Please Paula, I don't want to talk about what Dad did or didn't do. I know it might seem trivial to you, with Kit so ill, but I never got over my disappointment that she took you to Paris instead of me."

"Darlin', that was decades ago."

"Neurotic, aren't I?"

"No, not at all." She took a deep breath. "Kit knew how upset you were at being left behind. In Paris, she searched the shops for a beautiful and very expensive silk dressing gown. She wanted to give you something special."

I shook my head, bewildered. "I never got it."

The Lovely Nieces

"I'm afraid that your mum felt a silk dressing gown was too intimate a present for Kit to give to a young girl. Remember this was years ago, people were far more homophobic than they are now."

"What happened to the dressing gown?"

"Kit let her keep it. I chose a scarf for you from a boutique at the airport on our way home."

"I hated that scarf."

She grinned at me. "I knew you'd hate it but you see, I was jealous of *you*. Kit was always worrying about you, what a sad little soul you were, how you needed taking care of. Nobody ever saw me as a 'sad little soul' – even as a child, I was strong, reliable Paula."

I paid the bill and together we went out into late afternoon sunshine. I was heading back to the hospital, Paula was going home to make dinner for her daughter. Where our paths diverged we stopped and talked a little more. I asked her about Lydia, the love of Kit's life. The cousins had never met her but Kit had told them stories.

"Adventures really," Paula said. "Kit was heartbroken when Lydia died a few years ago."

Arriving at the hospital, I didn't go straight into the ward. Instead I sat outside in the gardens and tried to think. It seemed as if I'd spent my life, to date, being inattentive. How had I missed that my father had continued to orchestrate my life even from a distance? How had I missed that my dearest aunt was heartbroken?

I had a plan. I searched every toy shop in Shoreham and Worthing. I caught the train to Brighton. No luck. I visited junk shops, antique shops – charity shops as well. Finally, on my third trawl of Worthing, behind a large baby doll that cried and peed and had a vocabulary of ten words, including 'Mama' and 'Want a potty', I found what I was looking for.

There were no nieces about on the day I returned to the hospital. I had Kit to myself. She lay propped up in bed; her spectacles, still held together with tape, were set at an odd angle across her nose.

"Hello Kit!" I said very loudly so she couldn't ignore me.

She blinked. That was all.

"Kit, pay attention. *It's me*. Your glamorous niece!" I tweaked the sleeve of her pyjama jacket.

She turned her head away.

Discouraged, I walked over to the window. On the wide sill were dozens of Get Well Soon cards: flowers and hearts, fluffy dogs and pretty cats; a huge card from Noreen and family, "To my darling Aunt, with God's blessings." I read them all, from Janet and Margaret, Abi and Sylvia, Jack and Jill. So many names belonging to people I'd never know. My card was tiny – and in a way, in pride of place, pinned to the sash blind – a hand-drawn daisy with a smiley face at its centre: "Dear Kit, get well. Love always, Cathy."

I returned to the bed and pulled out the visitor's chair. From my bag I took a parcel and began to unwrap the bright paper. I drew out a colourful cardboard box and laid it on the bed, making a big production of opening the top of the box, peeping inside with delight as if seeing the contents for the very first time. I glanced at Kit. She'd pushed up her spectacles and was watching.

From the box I drew out a doll – my Lydia doll, her face newly painted, lips as red as the evening Kit first gave her to me. She had fresh yellow curls, and wore a new dress – hair and clothes found in a charity shop near West Worthing Station.

The Lovely Nieces

Fascinated, Kit stared and then suddenly, making a strange growling sound, she grabbed the doll from my hand.

"Careful," I said.

Ignoring me, she gently cradled the doll in the crook of her arm. With great tenderness she began to stroke the flaxen hair.

"It's Lydia," I said.

Kit nodded, her attention fixed on the doll's face. "There, there, darling," she said. After that her words became unintelligible, but I had a sense of crooning or cooing, the gentle sound that doves and pigeons make.

Eventually Kit fell asleep. The doll slipped down beside her and I moved it up to rest against the pillow. I felt no sense of achievement over Kit's reaction. I thought how much I disliked my haphazard, hurried life, where those who truly mattered were thrown only crumbs of attention. I thought of a younger Kit and her dynamism and intelligence. How little I knew of my aunt. And Lydia, the love of her life. And being forced to spend so much of that life apart. How had Kit managed to be so caring of us all?

The man in the photograph wears a dress suit, a bow tie and a cummerbund around his waist. On his head he sports a top hat tipped at a cheeky angle, belying his stern expression, which is emphasised by a dark, drooping moustache. He leans slightly towards the camera, both hands clasping the top of a walking stick.

Leaving my coffee behind, I take the photograph into Kit's study, where I know there is a magnifying glass. I sit on the desk rather than the leather chair, mainly because I can! Slowly and meticulously, I inspect the photograph. The man I assumed to be Edwardian or Victorian... He is neither. Nor is he a man. The wrist watch with its leather strap is modern.

There are Venetian blinds at the windows, which are double-glazed and surely framed with UPVC. I'm laughing now: at the photograph, at my stupidity. I turn the photo over. Nothing. I return to the soapstone frame and dismantle it again. I see the writing on the piece of hardboard which, in my usual tearing hurry, I missed earlier – tiny writing, ink fading – "Kit & Lydia," dated ten years earlier. Kit would have been sixty-five. Lydia – how old was she? Neither looks sixty-five. In their chosen costumes, they seem somehow ageless.

IV

The Three of Us

I choose a seat at the long table with my back against the wall. I am mindful of anyone who might be observing me, mindful of holding in my stomach so that I appear as slim as I once was.

It is an Indian restaurant, The Maharani in Brighton. A dinner to celebrate Paula's sixtieth birthday. How can she be sixty? The Paula I recognise in my head is a skinny running child. She has long brown legs, thin brown arms, sharp elbows jabbing left and right as she fights for possession of our battered football.

There are sixty guests, one for each year: friends, family, children and grandchildren. No children or grandchildren of mine. No husband or partner either, which nowadays suits me. As I sometimes say, in the hope of being contradicted, "At fifty-seven I'm no spring chicken." My brother Steven is a year older and his partner Ruth a year older still. I know Steven is equally mindful of how he appears. He might seem relaxed amongst the cousins but that is all an act.

The three of us, lined up against the wall, are polished and hairdressered, tanned and expensively dressed. We look far more prosperous than we really are. This illusion of prosperity is for the cousins' benefit. Although every one of them probably has more money than we do, *we* imagine that *they* imagine that Steven and I (Ruth is discounted because she and Steven have never married) are bordering on being – if not already are – multi-millionaires, based on the assumption that my late father had left us millions, or even billions. This blurred falsehood makes me uneasy. I believe Steven quite enjoys the fiction.

"Hello Cathy," my cousin Frank says, pulling out a chair for his third wife Betty on the other side of the table.

"Hello Frank." I smile across at him. At family gatherings it is always a relief to see Frank. He's hardly changed. Again, in him I see the wiry boy in the stocky, elderly man. I remember wet afternoons, drawing pictures at my aunt and uncle's battered kitchen table with Frank's sisters Paula, Noreen and Hazel.

"Frank, which drawing do you like the best?" Hazel always asking that same question, wanting her older brother's approval.

He'd study all four drawings carefully and then say, "Cathy's by a mile."

"It's not fair. You always choose hers."

Later, Hazel would pinch me or tear my picture or pull my hair. "He's our brother," she'd hiss. "Not yours."

I watch the three sisters as they welcome guests into the restaurant. Each has once been a beautiful child, teenager, young woman. They were so vibrant, so full of energy and curiosity, capable of achieving almost anything, yet none of them has done very much with their lives – or that is how we, the faux-rich cousins, choose to see them. For a while in her late teens, Paula modelled. As Steven will remark when we drive home later, Paula would still look stunning if she'd make more effort – her fine-boned face has hardly changed at all.

*

We were six and seven years old when Mum left our father. Eventually we ended up living with my cousins. *A refuge,* Mum called it. *Just a few months till we get on our feet.* It was never a refuge to me, and the few months turned into almost a year.

I remember how at first, Noreen – the oldest sister – combed and plaited my long hair, tied ribbons to my toes and fingers, made me feel pretty and dainty. Her attention didn't last. I was a doll Noreen got tired of playing with.

Of all our female cousins, Paula remains my favourite. Everyone loves her (except Ruth).

Hazel of the once Titian hair has put on the most weight. She dresses as if for a heavy seduction scene. As if at any moment she'll languorously sprawl out on a cushioned chaise longue and her clothes (draperies really) will slide away with an erotic shushing sound. Nude, Hazel would still look terrific to the connoisseur of the fuller figure, but she no longer has the confidence to sensuously insinuate her body into a room; instead she sails forth, head and shoulders held back to balance the extra weight of breasts and stomach.

This evening, to disguise her altered figure, she's wearing a white lacy throw over her chiffon dress. I groan inside; Hazel is making for our table. In her hurry to reach us, the fringe of the throw trails across the heads of seated guests.

"You look the spitting image of your old mum," Hazel yells from several feet away, which is like having cold water trickled over my head.

I've fought for most of my life to distance myself from my chilly mother. "Thank you, Hazel. That is possibly the worst greeting you could give me."

Hazel rests her hands on her hips and says defensively, "In her heyday, your mum was a raving beauty."

"A raving loony," I hear Ruth mutter to her piece of chapati.

"Before my time," I answer.

"Don't be ridiculous. You look just like her. That's her expression to a T."

"And what expression would that be?"

"Snooty!" Hazel cackles loudly. "Hello Steven, got a kiss for your cousin?"

Without waiting for a reply, Hazel leans across the table and plants a large purple kiss on his cheek. On my right I feel Ruth stiffen. I consider making a 'V' sign at Hazel but it is too early in the evening. Nobody is drunk. A 'V' sign might just look like very bad manners, so instead I shrug and bend my head over my empty plate.

"Fuck off, Hazel," Frank says cheerfully.

"Fuck off yourself," she says, and then fucks off.

Every time we meet, all three of my female cousins focus on my brother. Even their brother Frank thinks Steven is pretty smart. What is it Steven has? He can be all things to everyone. He is charming and charismatic, but it doesn't necessarily mean a thing.

Next to me, Steven is pontificating: his hands loosely linked under his chin; sleek, tanned head tilted to one side as if listening intently, instead of actually doing most of the talking. I'm aware that every bit of social intercourse Steven indulges in needs to be prepared for as if he is acting in a play. Possibly without realising, his aim is not to blend in but to stand out. This evening, because he considers our cousins provincial, he is playing at being a sophisticated European. Recently he's taken up smoking again, to show that he's bucked the trend to give up smoking.

He wears a dark blue cotton jacket bought in France. He

The Three of Us

refers to it as an 'artisan's jacket'. It cost very little. Under this is a black tee-shirt, well cut, with a Polydor record label screen-printed on the front (monochrome, nothing flashy), to remind the cousins that he was once something in the music business. Cream-coloured chinos, slim fitting. Steven carries no excess flesh. At home he has a sun bed which he uses with dangerous regularity, but his tan appears quite natural.

"So, how are you finding the retirement game?" Steven asks Frank.

"I'm loving it. Some people can't find enough to fill up their time. Not me."

"What do you do all day?"

I see that Steven is bursting to assert that he personally would never give up work, that he lives for his antique business, the banter, the comradeship of buying and selling, the reminiscing over deals done, the crystal chandelier worth a fortune that got away, the original Mucha print someone found in a skip and made a killing on.

Frank says with a shy smile, "We're going to line-dancing classes." He glances across at Betty. She nods but doesn't return his smile. Frank says, "It isn't just about Stetsons, cowboy boots and 'yee-haa-ing', it's a challenging dance. We learn LeRoc and jive as well. I was always pretty limber."

"Life's good then?"

"Almost couldn't be bettered. And I've taken on an allotment. I'm still doing odd gardening jobs around the estate. There's just one big cloud on my blue horizon, but I don't intend to let that spoil my evening."

Frank leans back in his chair and picks up his glass. I notice his hand is shaking and that although he loves red wine, tonight he is sticking to water.

Steven says, "Me, I've got my fingers in so many pies –" He

holds up his hand and begins counting off pies. I tune out.

I'm concerned about Steven's partner, Ruth. She can't stand the cousins or their progeny, or gatherings for birthdays in distant restaurants, with no idea by whom, where or when the bill will be paid. But Ruth seems okay. She is seated opposite Betty. Betty has changed – well, to a certain extent we've *all* changed. No matter how hard or how little we try, everyone looks as if they've had their bodies and features inflated with varying amounts of air.

Steven orders bottles of Cobra beer for the two of us, sparkling water for Ruth. More starters arrive at the table. It seems to be accepted practice that the men help themselves to the lion's share while the women talk and make sure the children are safe and happy. A dish of samosas is placed in front of me. I would like to eat the lot but Frank and Steven help themselves to four each and beam conspiratorially at each other.

I go to the loo and ascertain that yes, I do look pretty stunning, all things considered. Far better than I looked in my twenties. *Pretty good, girl,* I tell my reflection. And why not? Throughout childhood and most of my teens I was the ugly duckling.

These looks won't last much longer and I intend to make the most of them. It's the same for my brother. We've spent the first fifty years of our lives trying to turn ourselves into silk purses. From starting as two small kids owning less than nothing – a mother with not a maternal bone in her body, a father who was more than fatherly, we were the poor relations to be crowded into one small bedroom in the cousins' house – we haven't done so bad. Better than we could have ever hoped for.

*

Returning to the table, I'm aware that Ruth is flagging. Frank's gone walkabout. His wife Betty is talking but her eyes roam the restaurant for him. Frank likes to work a room. I've noticed this before. Frank is quiet but that doesn't mean he expects everyone else to keep quiet. He is content to position himself close to a group of his relations, listening and sometimes nodding. On rare occasions he'll interject a humorous comment or a few wise words, so that people turn towards him and take notice.

Distractedly, Betty tells Ruth, "I must... he really shouldn't... excuse me." She leaves the table.

Ruth looks at me before raising her eyes ceilingwards. "Betty's told me everything I'll ever need to know about her grandchildren. I hardly got a word in edgeways about my own. Where's Steven gone?"

"He's outside having a cigarette."

"Where's Paula or Noreen or Hazel?"

"Outside watching him have a cigarette."

"Once upon a time I'd have been furious. What does that signify?"

"That you trust him?"

"That I can't be bothered to do otherwise."

"Ruth, that's not true."

"Sorry. I just hate these bloody events."

"So do I."

"But you're good at them. Everyone talks to you."

"Erm yes – like Hazel saying I looked like Mum."

"You look nothing like your mum. Hazel's jealous because she's put on weight and nobody fancies her anymore. I'm going to the loo."

The main meal begins to filter through from the kitchen, bringing the guests back to their seats. This time I manage to commandeer more food and shut out the nagging voice warning me that I may appear greedy. My stomach has a magical quality of disappearing completely when I stand up but metamorphosing into a sizable tyre of flesh when I sit down. I adjust my napkin accordingly.

Just observing my cousins, their children, listening to stories they tell me about their lives, I experience a foolish, sentimental thought that maybe it would be nice to see more of them in the future. After all, we are related and doesn't that stand for something? But I keep my mouth tightly shut, ask nobody to visit. When Noreen points out that I only live an hour away by train, I reply that regretfully we are all so very busy.

"Such a pity." I shrug eloquently.

Back at the table, Frank is watching me. Our eyes meet with genuine affection. He smiles, then lowers his gaze.

It wasn't only him choosing my drawings that made me like Frank. I remember him, his voice gentle, telling everyone when my cousins teased me for not joining in their games, "Cathy's shy, that's all, isn't it, Cathy?" I'd nod and put all my gratitude into my eyes. But Frank wasn't there much. He was fourteen and hoping to sprint for the county.

Possibly due to the three beers I've drunk, I succumb to a desire to say one thing to one cousin that is true and even positive about that brief period of time in childhood when we saw each other every single day.

"Frank," I say.

"Yes?" He puts down his knife and fork and gives me his full attention.

As adults, Frank and I have probably never exchanged more than a hundred words. Each time our paths cross at these gatherings, we exclaim over how pleased we are to see

The Three of Us

each other before moving on to talk to someone else.

I lean forward. "You were the first person that I ever had a crush on."

Next to Frank, Betty looks surprised and then frowns. But what does that matter? I am talking about fifty years ago.

"Was I?" Frank looks delighted.

"When I was small, do you remember how all your sisters bullied me, even Paula? I was just a nuisance to them, but you were always gentle and very patient. It was as if you knew how frightened I was."

"I did know."

Like an overwhelming wave, other people's conversations wash over us. Our words become a bright blue plastic bag picked up by the tide and carried out to sea. When the wave disappears, I find myself talking across Steven to Paula about what books she is reading. Frank has resumed his tour of the distant relations. Betty and Ruth are now comparing snapshots of their grandchildren. Betty is winning. She's brought a photograph album the size of an encyclopedia with her.

I order another beer and get to my feet. I speak to Hazel's husband Alex and then to my cousins' children. This birthday celebration is different from the ones before. There are no really old people left. The last survivor from that generation, Aunt Kit, died two years ago.

Here in the restaurant, it is as if the contingent made up of our mums and dads, aunts and uncles have all been pushed off the top of a ladder and now there remain at least three empty rungs above us. Here we all are – me and Steven, Ruth and the cousins – huddled across the middle section, fearful of being forced upwards. Behind us are the children, and then a noisy, wailing cluster of grandchildren swarming over the lower rungs, still imagining climbing up a ladder to be just another jolly game.

I glance back to my table and meet Ruth's pleading eyes. "Help me!" she mouths. I return to my seat and immediately see that Paula has her hand on Steven's thigh. To Steven, Paula says, "So do you remember those sexy shenanigans we got up to in the garden shed?" Steven nods and grins.

For her birthday dinner, Paula has styled her hair into an approximation of a fashion not seen in Brighton since the 1940s, and dyed it a gingery red. She does look quite odd. But so do Hazel and Noreen. Years ago, when we were kids, I envied my cousins' dressing-up trunk full of silk and satin petticoats, tattered saris, shawls and jewellery, bequeathed by our Indian grandma. It is as if this habit of dressing up has stuck and none of them ever goes out with the intention of buying a complete matching outfit, or even a complementary outfit.

At every family event, all the stuff about the shed and sexual childhood games comes up. I feel more sad than irritated. Particularly Paula's life appears to have been defined by that one year when we lived in their house. I was never included in any 'sexy shenanigans'. It was eight-year-old Steven, the centre of secret, giggling games with his older girl cousins, in the shed, behind the clothes horse, up in the attic.

I look at Paula's hand. Not a young hand anymore, no scratches from picking blackberries, no mud under childish nails. Paula at sixty, still emotionally stuck. Twice married, two children, a present boyfriend. I can't envisage Norman as a 'lover'. At best, I uncharitably think Norman looks like a neighbour you wouldn't want too much to do with. Which I accept sounds snobbish, but aren't perfectly nice people, i.e. myself, allowed to have the odd snobbish thought? It *is* curious that I feel Paula is far too good for Norman but not good enough by a mile for *my* brother.

How would Steven have turned out if he'd married Paula? He'd never have let her leave the house with her hair that colour, or wearing a turquoise tartan skirt. Whatever tartan could it be? I sit forward so Ruth on my other side can't see Paula's hand resting on Steven's thigh.

"Yes, I do remember the shed," Steven says. Surely, he's told Paula that already?

Noreen calls across, "What about the clothes horse? You were a saucy little boy."

"Ha-ha, the clothes horse," chuckles Steven.

"Not the bloody clothes horse again," Ruth says tiredly. "Cathy, do you think we can go home soon?"

"I'll get the bill."

"Make sure we're not paying for anyone else."

"Will do."

To Steven, I say loudly, "We're going in a minute."

Paula wails, "Not yet. I've not spent half enough time with my boy." Getting to my feet, I kick Steven's chair hard so that he topples forward and Paula's hand is dislodged.

"Ruth, move into my chair," I say. "I think Steven wants a word."

It takes me some time to reach the cash desk at the back of the restaurant. So many cousins' kith and kin stop to talk. I'm aware that I'm popular with them in a way Steven isn't. Alex, Hazel's husband, puts a hand on my arm. He has reached the tearful stage of being drunk. "You do know about Frank?" he says.

"He and Betty have started line-dancing classes?"

"Cancer. Unbelievable. So unfair." As he reaches for a wine

bottle, I move away. Alex isn't someone I want to share my thoughts with.

At the till, the waitress seems thrilled to see me, but perhaps she is relieved that at last some of the guests are beginning to make tracks.

"The bill please," I say.

The waitress shakes her head. "No bill. All paid for."

"Surely not?"

"Yes, all paid for."

Paula materialises at my side. "It's my birthday. I'm treating everybody, darling."

"Paula, that's so generous."

We both look a little tearful.

"Thank you for bringing Steven. I know he wouldn't have come if you hadn't made him. He doesn't care enough –"

"Oh, but he does."

But of course, he doesn't. If I hadn't insisted, he and Ruth wouldn't have come. Yes, he laps up their admiration, Paula's affection and the dreams he reads in her eyes of what might have been, but not enough to drive for a couple of hours on a cold night.

"We knew *you'd* come," Paula says. "You always do."

"I always will."

Frank joins us. Suddenly, I'm aware of how frail he looks. He puts both his arms around my waist and draws me towards him. We are the same height, eye to eye. He smiles. That smile, lopsided, is the smile I remember. He says, "Cathy, why after all these years did you choose today to tell me I was your first crush?"

"It just seemed that I had to tell you, Frank. I didn't mean anything by it. I hope Betty isn't offended."

He ignores that. "Listen, I may have been *your* first crush, but I've had a crush on you for over fifty years. I've had a crush on you through three wives, four children and I don't know how many grandchildren."

We are both upset. There is nothing more to be said. Bad timing or just – timing.

"Take care, Franky." I kiss his cheek.

"And you."

I round up Steven, rout Ruth from the loo where she is repairing her eye makeup. "Your brother's a bastard," she says.

"He loves you. These few hours don't matter. They just flatter his ego."

"What about my ego?"

"Yes, I know."

Driving home, all three of us are quiet. Wordlessly, Ruth feeds Steven cans of Red Bull to keep him alert while driving. Halfway home and I see her hand move across the gears and rest in the exact spot on Steven's thigh where Paula's hand rested earlier. He gives Ruth a quick, smiling glance before turning his attention back to the road.

In my head I pick over the evening: my conflicted emotions around the cousins, the appositeness of choosing this night to tell Frank about my childhood crush, before I'd realised just how ill he was. I see Frank turning away – not going back to sit next to Betty or line dance or work on his allotment – his hand reaches up to the next rung on the ladder.

"Penny for them?" Steven throws over his shoulder.

"A depressing evening," I answer.

Ruth turns in her seat. "Cathy, whatever made you tell Frank you'd had a crush on him? Betty was furious."

"I was six years old at the time. Nothing for her to be furious about."

Steven says, "Overall I thought the evening went rather well. What say you, Ruth?"

"It was diabolical!"

"Was it?" Steven sounds astonished and then he starts laughing – a jolly boyish laugh which sets us all off. It is the relief really. To be going home. To be ourselves again.

LUCKY PATRICIA

I'd agreed to meet Meg for a late lunch at a wine bar in Stoke Newington Church Street. We'd be joined by our mutual friend Patricia and her new girlfriend, who were travelling by Eurostar from Paris. Patricia moved there several years ago for work and is the kind of woman who makes flying visits. Suddenly she's in the country and if I'm not quick about it, she's flown off somewhere else and I've missed her for another two years.

Patricia keeps in touch by round-robin emails, but not tedious ones. No *Monica's kittens are unbelievably cute* or *Guess what? We've succumbed to a gas barbecue!* Patricia's round-robins are full of sex and suicide. Nobody she knows ever just breaks up with their partner and walks off into the sunset; wrists are slashed, cars are trashed, vendettas form, litigation lasts, which brings excitement-at-a-safe-distance into my quiet life as a small-scale market gardener.

Eve, the new girlfriend, first surfaced about eight months ago; a brief mention when she joined Patricia's English-speaking lesbian book group. A fortnight later and she'd arrived at Patricia's studio flat in tears – at two am and with several large, expensive suitcases. Jeremy (Eve's husband) had "sworn on his mother's life to behead Eve with the axe he kept for chopping firewood".

"This man is the director of a multinational," Patricia wrote. "He's willing to jeopardise his whole career to wipe poor Eve off the face of the earth. Can you believe it?"

Well no, I hadn't quite believed it. My own thoughts were that he was probably just very annoyed with Eve, perhaps because she'd joined a lesbian book group, but once he calmed down, they would work things out over a nice meal and a bottle of good wine, which as a director of a multinational he could well afford. Or they might simply divorce and live happily ever after. I set aside the question of what the director of a multinational was doing chopping his own firewood in the first place.

By Easter, Jeremy had disappeared from Patricia's emails, but Eve was mentioned frequently. Eve smelt "like a bowl of expensive, ripe peaches". I liked the words 'bowl', 'expensive' and 'peaches', but was uncertain about 'ripe', but that could have been due to my horticultural background. 'Ripe' meant 'action stations', because quite quickly after ripe comes 'over-ripe'. Before I could dwell too much on this, another email arrived telling me (and all the rest of Patricia's friends worldwide) that Eve's underwear was "to die for".

"My personal favourites are her silk French knickers and camisole top ensemble in *eau de nil*," Patricia informed us. "Never in my life – even in gay Paree – have I met a woman wearing *eau de nil* underwear. Eat your hearts out, guys."

At that point Meg and I met up to compare reactions.

I said, "It would take far more than Eve's underwear ensemble to make me willing to kill myself on its behalf, Meg, although I must admit I have reassessed my own underwear drawer and found it wanting."

Meg frowned. "Lucy, I think you've missed the point here – what Patricia is actually telling us, is that she and Eve are now lovers."

"Are they?"

"Well how else would she know about Eve's underwear?"

"Perhaps she saw them drying over Eve's towel rail."

"Do rich people dry their underwear over towel rails?" Meg asked as if she really wanted to know.

Of course, Meg was right about them being lovers. By Christmas we had personal facts about Eve at our fingertips that we didn't know about each other – and Meg and I had been friends for nearly fifteen years. Quite apart from Eve's recent tattoo of the Tree of Life, its roots curling down between the "firm globes of her buttocks", Eve owned an apartment on the Côte d'Azur, a luxury chalet in the French Alps, a Lichtenstein, several Pollocks and an early Picasso. Since leaving Jeremy, Eve was apartment hunting, but she'd not found anything in her preferred area of the 7th Arrondissement (overlooking the Seine, Patricia wrote) with enough space to do her art collection justice.

I had a bad feeling about Eve that I didn't share with Meg, who tries very hard to be a glass-half-full woman, notwithstanding her rocky long-term relationship with Eileen, a local dog breeder. I think it was Eve's money that gave me the bad feeling. Well yes, it was definitely her money.

I'm not poor. Nor am I rich. I never will be. I hoped my bad feeling wasn't about envy, but more anxiety for Patricia's welfare. It seemed as if she'd attached herself to a jet plane (Eve). I visualised Patricia in a leather flying helmet and goggles, hanging on to one of Eve's sleek, gleaming wings, exhilarated, intoxicated, not realising the danger she might be in.

I found Meg already sitting in the wine bar, cradling a glass of white wine. She'd pulled up four chairs around an oval table near the door. Patricia and Eve were getting a cab across to North London and weren't sure of their exact time of arrival, so Meg had brought along two fleece jackets to put over the backs of the vacant chairs.

"It gets so crowded at lunchtime – I'd hate Patricia and Eve not to have seats."

"We could all stand at the bar."

"I can't imagine Eve would enjoy standing at the bar. She is a multi-millionairess."

"Is she?"

"If she owns real estate…"

Sometimes Meg's thoughtfulness amazes me. It goes well above and beyond normal thoughtfulness. Most of her day is spent devising little extra kindnesses for everyone, which often go unnoticed or unappreciated. Meg has a nice face. Her eyes are her best feature. They are brown and warm and, objectively, would look perfectly at home in a Labrador's head – which is possibly why Eileen the dog breeder took up with Meg in the first place.

Outside, it was a beautiful sunny April day, which made the interior of the bar seem particularly dark. We lit four tea lights.

"Welcoming," Meg said.

I was in good spirits and although Meg seemed a little down, we both agreed we were curious about Eve and it would be great to see Patricia again. I kept our conversation off the loathsome Eileen, who was having an affair with a woman called Joyce who bred Bedlington Terriers.

"I have to admit that they are lovely little dogs," Meg had told me earlier in the week, as if that were sufficient reason for Eileen to prefer Joyce, "like lambs."

"They're perfectly horrible little dogs – they're like lambs that have walked into a wall."

"Which makes them rather endearing, don't you think? Vulnerable."

There are moments when Meg is so sweet natured, I almost find myself applauding Eileen's bad behaviour.

I ordered a glass of white wine for myself and regaled Meg with tales of my new asparagus bed, my setback with Chinese artichokes counter-balanced by my outstanding success with dwarf cannellini beans.

"I've never heard of cannellini beans," she said admiringly.

"I'll let you have some of my seedlings."

"Perhaps we could swap – my courgette seedlings for your beans?"

I didn't really need Meg's courgette seedlings, but we agreed on a seedling exchange at the weekend over a glass of wine on my patio (weather permitting), which sounded quite fun. Days spent working with the soil are often rewarding but can get lonely.

Meg touched my arm. "They're here."

Patricia and Eve stood in the doorway as if reluctant to step out of the sunlight. The two of them formed an attractive tableau against the backdrop of quirky Stoke Newington shop fronts. They were exactly the same height, about five foot three, and they faced each other. Patricia was smiling at Eve and Eve was staring directly into Patricia's eyes in an adult kind of way.

Meg jumped to her feet and called out, "Hey, you two. Hurry up, we're starving."

I stood up as well and shouted, "Ditto."

They started laughing at something each saw in the other's eyes, then Patricia took Eve's hand and led her in.

Eve was very slender, very straight backed. She was probably nearing fifty but with not an ounce of extra flesh. I envied her her jaw line. I wondered if she'd had surgery but decided not. We lesbians don't often do surgery. Not that Eve looked like any lesbian I'd ever met. She made me think of a predatory bird or a very thin, sleek wolf. She wore jeans, leather Cuban-heeled boots, an expensive-looking puffa jacket with a drawstring waist – which as a rule flatters no one, but on Eve actually looked good.

Patricia helped her slip out of the jacket, draping it over Meg's fleece on the back of the chair. For all Eve's leanness, her figure was womanly; high, full breasts emphasised by the snug fit of her scarlet polo-neck.

"Thank you for that, darling," Eve said to Patricia as if hanging up her jacket had been at least as arduous as say, bringing life-saving water from a distant oasis. She sat down. We didn't sit. Patricia introduced us. It felt like being presented to royalty. I hopped nervously from one foot to another, not knowing whether to plant a kiss either on Eve's face or in the air around her face, or just drop a low curtsey. Finally, I settled on sticking my hands in the pockets of my trousers, smiling as widely as my lips would allow and nodding my head.

"Hey." Patricia punched me gently in the ribs.

"Hey." I hugged her.

"I've told Eve so much about you guys."

Meg and I beamed at Eve.

(I didn't respond with, "And Patricia's told us so much about you, Eve," in case Eve leant interestedly forward and asked, "Really? Exactly what?"

"Oh, just about your Tree of Life tattoo, your buttocks, your underwear and your husband wanting to behead you. The usual.")

Meg went to the bar and came back with a bottle of dry house white and four glasses, then went back for still bottled water and two water glasses because Patricia and Eve were still feeling "a little nauseous" from the repetitive movement of the train. While Meg poured wine and water and had to be restrained from going in search of ice cubes, I studied Eve.

Her hair was black, relieved by fine threads of grey. A perfect cut, a naturally wavy Greek-boy statue style. A garland of laurel would have been appropriate – or any garland. I found myself tracing the outline of Eve's top lip on the thigh of my trousers. Her lip was thin but again perfect, two peaks with a dip carved between. Sharp cheekbones, a fine nose with flared nostrils. Her eyes were bright blue. Not too many eyelashes, but those she had were mascaraed or perhaps dyed.

Eve began to talk exclusively about herself, bringing in Patricia for light comedy. She talked with absolute confidence, as if to a familiar audience. Nobody tried to halt the stream, not even to say, "Shall we take a look at the menu?" Eventually we did look at the chalk board above the bar, but only when Eve suggested it.

"Hey, I thought you were all hungry," she said, as if we'd been the ones doing the talking. Food was ordered. More wine for me and Meg; Eve and Patricia were now sticking to water.

Eve resumed her monologue. Patricia, usually such great company, sat turned towards her, enchanted by Eve's ability to follow one sentence with yet another. Sometimes Patricia looked searchingly into our faces, giving us her huge, slow smile, like we must be having such fun listening to this tremendous, extraordinary woman she'd found.

Eve talked about the new apartment she'd bought. She was project managing the alterations and decor.

"Eve's a brilliant seamstress," Patricia said proudly. "She's made all the cushions."

Eve told us about the cushion material being a William Morris pattern that picked up the colour of the curtains and the painted bookshelves. She said she was worried about Patricia's books because there were so many of them and they were all paperbacks and very dog-eared. Meg and I looked suitably worried on her behalf, although both of us had too many dog-eared paperbacks and were very fond of them. Eve said Patricia's taste in art was "absolute shit". We nodded and laughed as if we knew and agreed. Patricia laughed and nodded too.

"She's right. My taste is shit. Eve's going to teach me better taste."

I tried to catch Meg's eye but she kept her gaze fixed on Eve. Under the table I nudged her foot – she moved her foot away from mine. In my head I wondered if anyone would mind if I said, "I'm just going outside for a breath of fresh air." I'd hang around in the street doing some breathing and stretching exercises and then when everyone's attention had reverted to Eve, I'd slope off home. I wondered whether Meg might be thinking exactly the same thing, and how amusing it would be if we both, by some synchronicity, stood up and said, "I'm just going outside for a breath of fresh air."

"Am I missing the joke?" Eve asked.

I realised I was smiling when obviously I should have been looking concerned about something she was saying. I was saved from replying because Meg *did* suddenly leap from her chair and rush outside. Before I could leap up and join her, Eve was on her feet and through the door.

Patricia grabbed my arm. "Let Eve handle this, Lucy."

I sank back into my chair. "Handle what?"

"I think Meg's pretty unhappy at the moment."

"How do you know?"

Patricia spread out her hands. "Email. Meg writes every week."

Eve and Meg were coming back in, Eve's arm around Meg's shoulders.

"I'm sorry," Meg said, wiping her eyes with the back of her hand. Eve guided Meg to her chair as if she was incapable of making it unaided, then went to the bar and returned with another bottle of still water. She dropped a wad of paper napkins into Meg's lap and poured water into Meg's empty wine glass.

"This is what you need. Wine can be such a depressant."

Meg sipped the water, tears still streaming down her face. The bar was busier now with people coming in for early evening drinks; our table seemed to be the centre of furtive attention.

"I'm sorry," Meg said again, "you have no idea just how desperate I feel at the moment."

I caught a reproachful glance from Patricia. Obviously as Meg's friend I should have had some idea. What could I say? Yes, I did know Meg was desperately unhappy but thought she'd prefer it if we kept off the subject and stuck to a mutual love of the home-grown vegetable?

Meg mopped tears with the napkins but they kept on coming. I fumbled for her hand but found myself squeezing her shoulder bag.

"Let her cry," Eve said, "I've been there."

Which was annoying as I'd have liked to have got in first with my own "I've been there", not that it had occurred to me till Eve said it. Eve pulled her chair closer to Patricia's. She rested one hand on Patricia's thigh, the other she clasped around her glass of water. I noticed her jewellery: an impressive sapphire ring and a snake's eye gold band. I'd bet money that the snake's eye came from Patricia.

Eve said, "While Meg recovers, can I share something about my husband Jeremy?" She fixed her gaze intently on my face. "Lucy, the bastard frightens the life out of me."

Maybe it was because I was on my fourth glass of wine and had hardly eaten anything, what with all the listening and concentrating I'd been required to do, but I'd moved on in my thoughts from snake's eye to garden snakes and how they enjoyed lying in the sun, to whether that made them susceptible to hawks, which brought me back to Eve, really and truly resembling a bird of prey – but what bird? She was too diamond perfect to be an ornery buzzard, but nevertheless, with her sculpted features and way of sitting forward without allowing her shoulder blades to touch the back of her chair –

Eve frowned at me. "Lucy, did you hear what I just said?"

Fortunately, over many years I have perfected the ability to listen quite closely to a conversation while also daydreaming. "You said, 'the bastard frightens the living daylights out of me.'" However, my intonation was obviously faulty because she looked queryingly at Patricia.

"It's okay, Eve. That's just Lucy's way. She often looks distracted but she's one hundred percent on the ball. Am I right, Luce?"

I nodded and tried to look "one hundred percent on the ball". Eve leant back in her seat and began. "As Patricia's probably told you, I have two lovely daughters. I love my kids. Hurt them, you hurt me. He wrote them a letter –"

At the tables around us, I was aware that the conversations had slowed and quietened – Eve's gaze flickered around the room as if ensuring she had an attentive audience. She paused, took a sip of water, "In it he said that Patricia was giving it to me... up the arse. Can you imagine how that made me feel, Lucy?"

I experienced an overwhelming, inappropriate desire to laugh, which I knew would be a disastrous response. I picked up a spare serviette and blew my nose heartily while surreptitiously sucking on the bottom section. I took my time scrunching the serviette into a ball and tucking it into my sleeve.

"How old are your daughters?" I asked.

She turned her killer blue eyes on me. "That's immaterial."

"Yes," Patricia agreed, "that is *totally* immaterial. The fact is that, true or false, he wrote that in a letter to his own children. Jeremy is a disgusting individual."

"He does sound awful," Meg said. Her tears had stopped.

"An understatement, Meg," Patricia replied, but not reprovingly like she'd sounded with me.

"I just wanted to share that with you both. You in particular, Meg, so you know that I feel your pain."

Meg flapped her hands apologetically. "Honestly Eve, I've got nothing to complain about that doesn't happen to someone somewhere every day; a girlfriend gets a new girlfriend – wants to move her in and," she gulped, "me out. I'll have to live with Mum, which means that I'll end up being her carer, which means I'll have to give up my job, which is no sort of a job really, but it suited me."

Patricia laid her hand on Meg's shoulder and squeezed. "You're having a tough time."

"No, no. Nothing as bad as Eve and her husband."

"Ex-husband any day now, the bastard."

Soon afterwards the party broke up. We stood outside on the pavement to say our goodbyes. Eve gripped Meg's elbows. "You visit us the next time you're in Paris."

"I'll do that," Meg said, as if she were frequently hopping on trains and planes.

I sensed a coolness towards me coming from Eve and Patricia. Somehow I knew I wouldn't be asked to visit them in Paris, and I wasn't. A cool kiss on the cheek was all I received from Eve; an arm squeeze from Patricia, but combined with a look of puzzlement in her eyes as if I'd proved a disappointment.

I watched them stroll away, just their fingertips linked. At a new luxury bath-product shop, they paused and peered in the window. I wasn't surprised. Eve was definitely a luxury bath-product person and soon Patricia might become one as well. I turned to share this insight with Meg as she emerged from the bar, her two spare fleeces over her arm.

"I left them behind." She gave me a watery smile. "Well, wasn't that nice?"

I said, "Actually, Meg, it wasn't nice at all. Eve is totally self-absorbed. She'll suck all the life and exuberance out of Patricia and eventually dump her for a fresher, wealthier model. I give them two years."

For the first time ever I saw Meg angry, her eyes hot and fierce, her breathing coming in quick, loud gasps.

"*You* give them two years?"

"Okay, five years. Certainly not forever. I'd say a limited time-line."

Meg's eyes, eyebrows, nose and mouth configurated into one huge sneer. "And what do *we* have to put next to their two years? Next to their 'limited time-line'?"

"Steady on, Meg."

"Two years of getting older on my own, looking after my mother, trying to avoid bumping into Eileen and her new girlfriend walking their dogs in Clissold Park."

"That's how you feel now, but I promise a day will come when you start looking forward again."

"Looking forward?" Meg shouted. "Eve and Patricia will have more to look forward to than exchanging courgette seedlings for runner beans."

"Cannellini beans. Well I'm sorry you don't find our exchange of seedlings very thrilling, I foolishly imagined it might be fun."

"I'm in love with Patricia," she spat out.

"With Patricia?" I echoed.

I felt like a small rodent in a box of sand searching for an appropriate sentence, certain I'd left a juicy one somewhere containing the elements of 'immoderate crying when apparently in love with someone else, Eileen, Bedlington Terriers, lack of trust combined with secretive and underhand behaviour'.

"Don't worry, Lucy," Meg almost snarled. "I don't intend to dump any of this on you, I just wanted to say the words to someone."

I wound my way back along the road towards Clissold Park and found an empty bench looking out over the lake. The late afternoon sun had turned the water to gold. Perhaps I should have been worrying about Meg, or regretting the possible loss of an old friend, but in fact I felt full of peace.

I imagined Patricia and Eve on the Eurostar train, shoulders touching, both wearing their expensive sun glasses even though the light was fading. Eve was possibly thinking, "Hmm, that went off pretty well. Now I don't need to meet these friends of Pat for at least another five years, if ever."

Lucky Patricia. Was I in love with her as well? I was certainly fond of her, but at that moment a little less fond, to coincide with her obviously feeling a little less fond of me. I'd never have the courage to fall for a woman like Eve, but was

I perhaps in love with Meg? No – although for several years I'd nurtured a soft spot for Eileen. Perhaps I should consider buying a dog, but not a Bedlington Terrier or a Labrador.

Was I a tiny bit in love with myself? Now that was a possibility. I'd always felt encouraged by the line from the Whitney Houston song about learning to love yourself being the greatest love of all.

Back with Eurostar, I visualised Patricia taking Eve's hand. "I'm so sorry about Lucy. She's changed. I'm thinking about deleting her from my round-robin mailing list."

"She seems a little weird, but don't do anything on my account."

Patricia twists the snake's eye ring that cost her a week's money. "You were just wonderful. The way you took care of Meg. I so appreciate it."

"Darling, it was nothing," Eve says.

They kiss. The dark lenses of their sun glasses tap against each other as the train speeds into a tunnel.

FOR THE LOVE OF ESTELLE

Today I have an hour to spare before my taxi arrives to take me to Zakynthos Airport. I'm sitting with a coffee at a wrought-iron table, watching the colour of the sea change from the greeny-grey of early morning to vibrant blue.

I am one of a dying breed, the woman who happily holidays alone. The woman who has stayed in the same apartment, at the same resort, during the last two weeks of June year after year – or at least I *was* that woman. There are other regulars like myself. Only a handful, but each summer we exchange greetings – not as long-lost friends, but as an acknowledgement that once again we have remained faithful to this enchanted spot on a Greek island.

Perhaps to the locals we represent a fixed sum of euros: ten for sun bed and umbrella, another ten for lunch, fifteen to include a bottle of village wine in the evening. But I hope I'm seen as more than that – almost, if not quite, one of them.

Now, let me introduce you to Tassos, the owner of the only taverna, my apartment and several others along this strip of coast. The sun bed and umbrella concession, possibly even the beach, belong to him. He is a person of some importance in this small community and I believe him to be a good and decent man. Throughout the summer days, Tassos favours a uniform of clean and ironed, knee-length combats, with short-sleeved tee-shirts in pale green or grey. After all these years, his hair remains thick and brown, cut short while retaining some wave. To say the least, he is taciturn, yet between him and me conversation, although sparing, has always been amiable.

"Okay?" Tassos will ask, a faux-leather menu tucked under his arm.

"Couldn't be better," is my invariable reply.

My order committed to memory, he'll nod, take one step backwards before walking in a slow amble towards the bar and then on to the kitchen. At the end of my meal I will make the gesture of scribbling on the palm of my hand and he will present the bill, although from experience I know the exact amount to the nearest cent.

I have the money plus tip ready for him. "Thank you, Tassos."

"*Parakalo*," he'll answer. "You're welcome." At this point his lips twitch into the merest hint of a smile.

Ten years ago, when I first arrived at this holiday destination, my initial impressions weren't favourable. I'd been hoping for a quiet village, but nothing quite so quiet! When the taxi dropped me off at seven am, the village was completely still and silent... and then a cockerel crowed. At the time I took its cry to be a bad omen, but on the contrary, any omen proved to be good. By evening, having unpacked and settled into my apartment, I located Tassos' Taverna and Bar, set on the clifftop overlooking the sea. As I mounted the steep stone steps from the beach, the fairy lights – strung out on ropes of electric cables in the olive trees – began to glow. I felt my shoulders relax and my mood swing from dark to hopeful.

Of all the bars in all the world, well, Tassos' is hard to beat. The food is okay. Sometimes, depending on who the chef is for the summer, it can be brilliant. On that first visit, the taverna had a sandwich board boasting 'Finest European Cuisine'. That board is long gone. Nobody comes here looking for Finest European Cuisine. We come because the place isn't just unspoilt, it is a microcosm of how we would wish our everyday lives to be: simple and delicious with an underlying sense of connection between moderate comfort and the earth, sea, and star-filled night. We know the times when the cicadas start and stop.

The terrace that first evening was almost empty. I sat down at a table and took out my novel and spectacles case – the armoury of the single woman on holiday.

Tassos arrived to take my order.

"Just a Mythos for now," I said, opening my book. I tried to read the first few pages but the sea and the sunset called to me. As I raised my head, I saw that between my table and the spectacular view sat a woman, Estelle Ferris – although at the time, of course, I had no idea of her name.

I judged her to be in her early forties. Her hair was shoulder-length and an extraordinary shade of rich red. (It might be helped along by a salon but I don't think so. Estelle has that milky-cream complexion that so often goes with red hair.) She resembled... and oh dear god, this is a poor and foolish thing to say about any woman, but it was a tigress. A splendid wild cat. And now I fear my hyperbole gets worse – forgive me, because even then I think I loved her – a splendid but cruelly injured wild cat. She took my breath away!

On the table in front of her lay an open notepad. I could see that she'd drawn a cobweb starting at the margin of her page and working inwards, becoming more complicated, extending into fresh cobwebs.

I remember thinking how very sad she looked, that her face appeared somehow newly haggard, and then she glanced in my direction. I saw such bewildered pain in her eyes.

"Your beer." Tassos placed the glass next to my book.

"Thank you," I said.

At the top of the beach steps, a couple appeared. They were smiling, pleased at what they'd found. Solemnly, Tassos approached them.

"Are we too late for dinner?" the man enquired. He had an American accent.

Tassos shook his head. He led them to a table next to mine.

"We kinda wanted a sea view, didn't we, Bill?" the woman said. They both looked meaningfully towards the empty tables on each side of the red-haired woman.

"They're reserved," Tassos said.

Later he brought the red-haired woman a plate of hummus, salad and pitta bread.

"Tassos, I don't think I can," she said.

"Try." He nudged the plate towards her.

I judged Tassos to be a few years younger – perhaps in his late thirties. Was he in love with her? As a possible couple they wouldn't have matched at all, but even then, not knowing anything about either of them, I sensed a fine binding thread.

Later, I heard the American couple talking. The wife said, "Bill, I don't believe those tables were reserved."

He grinned at her. "It's all Greek to me."

They both laughed.

I went to the bar and paid. As I passed the woman's table, I noticed that the pad with the cobweb drawing had been put away. I could see it tucked into her beach bag. The plate of food remained untouched.

*

For the Love of Estelle

Tassos had a wife but, as far as I knew, no children. The wife was small and dumpy and invariably wore a black dress with a white apron. She served at the bar and rarely came out onto the terrace except to clear the tables and snuff out the candles at the end of the evening. They seemed to get on well enough although they rarely spoke to each other, but then they rarely spoke at all. She didn't match Tassos either, but the difference was less marked.

Only recently the thought has occurred to me that it isn't always possible to perceive the matching of minds. Only recently it has also occurred to me that I am a thick-headed fool, but that becomes apparent later in my story.

Three years ago, Tassos' wife died. I didn't learn this till my following holiday, when a large painting in a gold plaster frame appeared behind the bar. It was a very inept rendering of a glamorous woman wearing a black scarf around her head. In script at the bottom of the frame, in both Greek and English: *Dionysia, beloved wife of Tassos*.

Tassos watched me as I leant forward to read the inscription.

"I'm so sorry," I said. "I didn't realise that your wife had died."

He shrugged. "Do you want a beer?"

"Yes. Thank you." I held out five euros but he waved my money away. I'd wanted to say something more about his loss but somehow, I knew that was it. I'd said enough.

This year, Tassos has been dressing more smartly. It is clear to me that he's having a mid-life crisis. On some evenings his cargo shorts have been replaced with dark denim jeans; tee-shirt changed for a crisp white shirt, with several buttons undone and the sleeves folded neatly to just below his elbows.

His hair is not quite the colour it was last June: there is now a dark burnish to his clipped waves, but I know I haven't imagined the grey threads that appeared in the last two years. He has shown no embarrassment about these changes and we – I – pretend that Tassos is as inscrutable and imperturbable as ever.

He has altered his work schedule. In the mornings he is no longer behind the bar. His cousin Toula now oversees the breakfasts, coffees and early morning ouzos. I like her. She speaks a little English and between the two of us there exists a small but happy conversation, surprisingly, around vegetables.

Her family have one of the allotments. (That isn't what they're called here.) They grow food to supply the mini-market and have done so for over twenty years. Two evenings a week, she works on the land; the succulent beef tomatoes that appear in the taverna's salads are her particular interest.

Tassos arrives around mid-afternoon. I asked Toula how long he has been coming later in the day.

"This season only. It's his age. He needs his beauty sleep." She grinned at me, then touched her lips with her index finger.

"I'm saying nothing." I smiled at her.

Naturally, the beautiful Estelle Ferris has grown older, but to me, her eyes are as fine, her nose as straight, her lips are still full and red. The few changes are, in my opinion, only for the good. Estelle no longer draws cobwebs or seems unhappy. She reads both English and Greek newspapers now and she smokes – black Sobranie cocktail cigarettes.

"Only on holiday, Georgina," she has told me. "A treat to myself."

We have eaten breakfast together on her balcony most days. We've shared a beach umbrella and talked and laughed. I like to think she was enjoying my company. If I'm honest,

Estelle has been the reason I've returned here year after year – and I write that with no pleasure at all. I have been grateful for every moment spent in her company, but these fragile memories have had to last me during all the remaining bleak and lonely weeks in between.

We both live in London and yet I couldn't bring myself to suggest meeting even for coffee. She too seemed hesitant, as if she knew our friendship wouldn't survive the cold climate of home.

For someone like myself – awkward and unconfident – loving another woman is a painful, unsatisfying experience. I envy younger women. They seem so fearless.

And how were matters between Estelle and Tassos? I didn't ask but I assumed much about their relationship. At some point, I concocted a lover in Estelle's past who had died or at the very least broken her heart. I imagined that despite being married, Tassos had stepped in to pick up the broken pieces.

A few late, hot evenings in the bar, when the only customers left were several sinuous cats and myself, I observed them both, sitting together at her usual table near the cliff edge, a bottle of wine between them, a candle burning steadily in the still air. Their voices were no more than a murmur, the monotone of old friends rather than lovers. I admit to feeling bitter and angry. I spent each day with Estelle and yet in all this time, she'd never invited me to sit at her table on the terrace, never invited me to even share a coffee at the end of an evening meal. These privileges were reserved for Tassos.

One week ago, I watched from the taverna terrace as Estelle made her way along the beach towards the stone steps. She smiled up at me and waved.

"How was the boat trip?" I called down.

"Wonderful. You should have come."

"The next time." I returned to my table.

As Estelle stepped onto the terrace, Tassos hurried forward and pulled out her chair. He took the reserved sign from the table. Normally, even when the taverna is busy, he stops for a few words with her, but this particular night he was distracted. At a table near the bar a woman sat. Her hair – so light a blonde to seem almost silver – reached to her waist. I supposed her to be Scandinavian.

"A glorious evening," Estelle said, smiling up at him. "The very air does me good."

Tassos forced his gaze away from the woman. He said, "Can I take two of your cigarettes?"

She looked puzzled, then playful. "Have you started smoking again?"

"The cigarettes – yes or no?" His voice was cold. Not hostile but as if he were asking something of a stranger.

"Of course." She flipped the carton open. "Take what you want. I thought you'd have cigarettes behind the bar."

"These are better." He helped himself to two cigarettes and hurried across the terrace. Estelle and I exchanged surprised looks. Neither of us had ever seen Tassos hurry anywhere before.

Tassos planted himself in front of the blonde woman's table, in such an odd, self-conscious way. It isn't easy for anyone to maintain an upright position with their legs crossed. On his left leg – the pillar leg – the cuff of his jeans was slightly pulled up by the weight of his leaning ankle and I could see he wore white socks with his polished brown loafers. Somehow, although I confess to knowing little about male fashion styles, I felt that out here in the Mediterranean, all a man needed in a leather loafer was a bare tanned foot.

He laid a cigarette each side of her wine glass. "Black Russian," he said. "Cocktail cigarettes. Very special. Very expensive."

The young woman looked pleased but also embarrassed. She reached for her handbag. Tassos frowned theatrically. "They are a gift from me to you. Now, lovely lady, what can I get you from our evening menu?"

On my right, a movement from Estelle distracted me. She was taking a novel from her beach bag, also a pair of spectacles.

I smiled across at her. "I didn't know you wore glasses."

She laughed. "Georgina, I'm not getting any younger."

I was right. The woman, Inga, was Swedish. Over the following few days it became obvious that Tassos was besotted by her. He remained attentive to Estelle but there was a sense that he was only going through the motions. Estelle would remark on a cat that was patently *enceinte*, chiding him gently for not neutering the male cats that hung around the bar. He would smile or laugh – this taciturn man who never smiled or laughed was putting on an act to impress Inga and not us.

He'd pause at my table. "Is the food to your liking, mademoiselle?" This, I think, was the altered Tassos' idea of a joke. Out of sheer embarrassment and regard for him, I forced myself to go along with it.

"It is indeed, Tassos. As always." Had it been possible for me to produce a girlish giggle, I would have done so. Unintentionally, the young woman was encouraging him to make a complete fool of himself.

Tassos did his best to be subtle, only sitting down with Inga once she'd finished eating. As if just pausing to catch his breath, he'd flop onto that second chair and there he'd remain until she rose to leave. I also noticed that he no longer presented the bill for her meal.

One afternoon on the beach, as we lay side-by-side on sunbeds, Estelle said, almost to herself, "I hate to see Tassos so desperate."

Imagining how hurt she must be feeling at his defection, I tried to reassure her. "Nothing will come of it. A beautiful young woman like that isn't interested in someone old enough to be her father."

"Do you think they're sleeping together?"

"Surely not." I glanced towards Estelle, expecting to see sadness in her eyes. As if to pre-empt me, she slipped on her sunglasses.

"Whether he's sleeping with her or not, he's going to get hurt," she said.

"Then he should show more sense."

Estelle laughed at me. "Georgina, don't you know what it's like to be infatuated? Being sensible doesn't come into it."

I could have given her several answers – all of them embittered. Instead, I stood up and walked into the sea.

In all these years, Estelle has never left the taverna before ten. Each evening, I'm always the first to wend my way home, but at nine o'clock the next night she gathered up yet another novel, her beach bag and her pashmina. At the top of the steps she hesitated and looked across at Tassos, sitting at Inga's table, his back turned to us.

"Tassos, I'm catching the early morning flight tomorrow," she called out.

I got to my feet, shocked. Surely Estelle had at least three more days left of her holiday? I wanted to cry out but, as always, the man and the woman took first place with their exchange.

Reluctantly, he turned his chair and held up his hand. "Go safely, my friend."

Wildly, I looked from him to her. Was that it? Ten years of friendship, a probable affair, reduced to *'go safely, my friend'*?

Leaving money for the bill next to my side plate, I followed Estelle. On the bottom step she'd paused to take off her sandals.

"Estelle, wait."

She looked up at me. "I'm going to paddle," she said. "The water's so warm."

"He's a pig," I hissed. "How could he be so rude? So careless."

"I expect Tassos feels time is running out for him," she said.

"Time is running out for us all." My voice was almost a snarl.

Estelle stood in the shallows, the skirt of her dress held up to above her knees.

"And why are you leaving early?" I couldn't keep the anger from my voice. "I think you could at least have told me."

"My mother's ill. I only heard this morning and I didn't want to spoil our day on the beach. I intended to leave a note."

I mumbled something stupid along the lines of, "You have no idea how upset I am." After all, who was I to be upset? A holiday friend – of no importance.

Carrying her sandals in one hand she re-joined me on the sand and together we began to walk back towards the apartments. There was no moon that night. Estelle took my arm. "Can I hang on to you?"

We'd never touched except by accident. The pressure of her hand made my skin feel as if it was burning.

"Georgina," she said. "There is something I think you need to know."

It was coming. How she loved him, would always love him

no matter how many women he became infatuated with, no matter what...

"The summer when you and I first met, my relationship in London had just broken up," she began. "I'd already been on the island a week trying to sort myself out. Tassos was kind to me."

"Because he was in love with you." My voice was harsh.

"I think you believe everyone is in love with me." She squeezed my arm. "Tassos and I are friends and that is all we've ever been."

"Then why do you keep coming back here, year after year?"

She countered. "Why do you?"

Leaving the beach, we stopped under a street lamp while Estelle slipped on her sandals. "Georgina, let's meet for a drink one evening – when we're both back in London."

I was still angry and confused. "Wouldn't that be very boring for you?"

She laughed, so heartily. I was glad it was dark, that she couldn't read the expression in my eyes. Then she stopped laughing. Lightly she touched my cheek with her fingertips, she traced the outline of my lips.

I waited.

Seconds passed. "That relationship," she lowered her head onto my shoulder, "was with a woman."

I waited.

"Each year I hoped you'd say something, make a move – but you never did."

I waited.

"Why didn't you?"

"Why didn't *you*?" But I needed no reply. It seemed like the most natural thing in the world for me to lock my arms around her.

*

Today, Tassos stands in front of me, a faux-leather menu tucked under his arm. "Okay?"

"Couldn't be better. And you? You're not usually around at this time of the morning."

He shrugs. "Inga is flying back to Sweden this afternoon. I'm driving her to the airport."

"Will you miss her?"

"A little. She says she'll come back next summer, but who knows? We all need some passion in our lives before we die." His lips twitch into the merest hint of a smile. "Don't you think, Georgina?"

Everyone in this village seems to know my name, but Tassos has never used it before. My eyes prickle with tears.

"Go safely, my friend," he says.

"Thank you, Tassos."

He raises the menu to his forehead and salutes me. "*Parakalo.* You're welcome."

OH YOU PRETTY THING

Part 1

Mark and Julie wear matching fifteen-carat gold wedding rings. Julie has an engagement ring as well: a diamond – small but real – in a platinum setting. After she'd been working at INFO-PULSE (a small marketing company a mile away from where she lives in Hemel Hempstead) for a few weeks, Donna, the office manager, asked her how long she'd been married.

"Seven years," Julie said.

Donna was amazed. "Julie, you look about eighteen. Marriage must suit you."

Julie flashed her a smile. "Yes, it does."

Actually, it only sort of suits her. If she had to give marks out of ten, it would probably be a four, although were she to ask Mark, he'd say, "Ten out of ten, no question!"

Okay, things Julie likes about being married: being addressed as Mrs Norman instead of just Julie Foster, bringing the words 'my husband' into most conversations, going shopping at the weekend with her 'husband' – Waitrose in Berkhamsted for groceries, and the recently opened Marlowes Shopping Centre for clothes and a meal. Oh yes, and the dog, first wedding anniversary present from Mark, a cocker spaniel. Julie named him Ziggy.

Oh You Pretty Thing

"After David Bowie's Ziggy Stardust?" Mark said, having been a fan of the album as a teenager.

Julie shook her head. "No, I just like the name."

Both Mark and Julie enjoy the preparation they put into getting ready to go out on Saturday mornings. Mark in particular wants them – as a couple – to look stunning; to eclipse and dazzle their neighbours as they slide into his three-years-old but gleaming-like-new Ford Sierra Coupé. Mark is an electrician. He likes his job. It brings in money but being an electrician isn't how he pictures himself long term. His ambition is to be his own boss, with Julie at home, central to his world.

One Saturday in particular sticks in Julie's memory. At the time, there seems nothing special about the morning. Only later, years later, when Julie reminisces with a mixture of sadness and relief (but never regret) will she see it as being significant.

Julie is admiring her reflection in the mirrored double doors of their fitted wardrobe, turning this way and that, thinking that not every woman can carry off ice-blue skin-tight jeans in a size ten worn with a baby-pink crop top. She turns to Mark, who is absorbed in colour-coding his sock drawer, and says, "I don't look too bad, do I?"

"You look fantastic."

"Did I ever tell you I was the most unpopular girl at my school?"

"You did."

"I'd never go to a school reunion but just sometimes I think I'd enjoy seeing everyone's faces when I arrive. Really, I'd like to be dead and floating above them and then see myself walk in the assembly hall and everyone looking surprised."

Mark gazes at her with admiration as if she's said something really profound. "Babe, I don't want you dead, but I'd love to be with you at that reunion." He joins her reflection in the mirror. "You know, Julie, these are our best years. We've got to make the most of them because they'll never come again."

It is Julie's turn to regard Mark admiringly as if *he's* said something really profound.

"How long will they last, Marky?"

"You'll look lovely when you're ninety."

"That will do me."

The following Monday at work, she repeats Mark's theory about their 'best years' to Donna, expecting her to be equally impressed. Instead Donna slaps her forehead and says, "What a load of bollocks, Julie. Sometimes, you make me want to vomit."

Donna has shortish brown hair with really bad purple highlights. In Julie's opinion, Donna isn't exactly fat, because she goes regularly to a gym, but if she hadn't gone to a gym then Julie probably would class her as fat because overall, Donna is what Julie might call a 'big solid woman'... meaning fat.

Donna dresses badly: cargo trousers – yuck! Jeans with cowboy boots – double-yuck! Shirts that make it obvious she isn't wearing a bra – a million trillion yucks! In twenty years' time when Donna's boobies are dangling round her waist, Julie knows she'll regret that no-bra decision.

Another thing, Donna is always anti-something: anti–sexual discrimination, anti–poll tax, anti–cruise missiles, anti-… depressants?

Once Julie asks her, "Donna, are you *for* anything?"

"Oh yes," she answers. "I'm for freedom of speech, abortion

on demand, social and gender equality, the National Health Service..."

Julie wishes she'd kept her mouth shut.

Mark wonders if Donna might be a lesbian.

"No Mark, she's a feminist," Julie explains. "If she'd been gay, she'd have made a pass at me by now, wouldn't she?"

In many ways, the young couple are unaffected by events taking place in the wide world, or even locally. They met in their teens, were engaged for six months, got married, rented a flat, then, with the help of Mark's parents, put a deposit down on a semi-detached Victorian cottage with some renovation work required.

"Only superficial problems," Mark's dad – a master bricklayer – said. "Nothing I can't put right for you."

Mark told Julie, "It's not our forever home, babe, but it will do for the time being."

Mark and Julie. Julie and Mark. Married couple with house, car and dog. Happy in their own small world. Indivisible.

Every other weekend, Julie and Mark visit his parents for a Sunday roast, which *is* quite tasty, but then his mum has been cooking roasts every single Sunday for as long as Mark can remember. The Sunday following Mark's 'best years' comment – after shoulder of lamb, roast and boiled potatoes, three different vegetables, gravy and mint sauce – his mum brings out a supermarket trifle in a plastic container. Julie is surprised because usually (as in, every Sunday for as long as *Julie* can remember) the pudding is home-made fruit crumble with double cream.

As Mark's mum peels back the cellophane cover, she smiles mischievously at her daughter-in-law: "You'll love this, Julie. I saw it in Sainsbury's and thought of you."

Reminding someone of a Sainsbury's fruit trifle isn't exactly complimentary. Julie raises her eyebrows. "Because?"

Under the table, Mark gives her foot a warning nudge.

"The pink cherries on top. You remind me of a pink cherry."

Which isn't exactly a compliment either. Under the table, Mark's foot presses down more firmly.

Julie winces before saying sweetly, "Mum, it looks delicious."

Mark awards her a look of great tenderness, as if she is a young and extremely attractive version of Mother Teresa.

In the car driving home, Julie says, "Mark, when your mum said I reminded her of a pink cherry, couldn't you have come up with a compliment for me rather than bruising my toes?"

He grins. "Babe, cherries are okay. If she'd said you reminded her of a prune, then I'd have said something. Anyway, I thought the trifle made a pleasant change. Didn't you like it?"

They pull into the driveway. Julie is the first out of the car. Inside the house she can hear Ziggy's barked welcome. Over her shoulder she calls back, "What's to like about fake cream and one glacé cherry each?"

Mark follows her into the house. "Julie, I don't like to hear you criticise my mother. I'm disappointed in you." He switches on the TV news, which he never usually bothers with – and wouldn't you know it, they are in the middle of an item on a famine somewhere like Somalia. Normally when there are famines or disasters on TV, Mark yawns and changes channels, but this time he gives Julie a meaningful, resentful look.

She says, "What do you want me to do? Buy up all the fake fruit trifles I can find and ship them abroad?"

Oh You Pretty Thing

Mark turns off the television, grabs his car keys, walks out of the room, out of the house, into the car, and off he drives.

Sometimes, Julie daydreams – not with any malice – that Mark will have a fatal accident. Nothing too gory like, say, the car and Mark's mangled remains found scattered at the bottom of a canyon (not that there are any canyons in or around Hemel Hempstead); but a possible pain-free heart attack would not be a total tragedy. Their mortgage will be paid off by Mark's life insurance, with enough money left over for Julie to give up work forever. So, as she listens to Mark's car roaring into the distance, she allows herself a tiny flicker of hope.

"Horrible, aren't I?" she says to Ziggy.

Ziggy's tail waves frantically.

Well no, not really, because as much as Mark loves her, he does always have the upper hand. Whenever Julie takes the time to think, having the upper hand is a side to Mark's father she doesn't like at all. Although she never says. Never dares to say. Mark's dad wears sleeveless pullovers over white shirts with the sleeves rolled up, which is innocent enough, but he reminds her of the dad in the 1970s film *Spring and Port Wine* she watched with Mark one wet Saturday afternoon. Mark had admired the stern yet kindly James Mason while *she'd* wanted his wife to get a divorce and find someone younger.

"But she loves James Mason," Mark insisted.

"She doesn't have any choice. And the children are totally browbeaten."

They didn't actually have a row but there was tension.

Just after ten, Mark comes back from his car ride. By then she's found a photo of him from their wedding album just in case she needs to alert Missing Persons. He looked so handsome in his wedding suit, with his thick black hair and brown eyes. Julie has fair hair and pale blue eyes. She isn't beautiful to match Mark's good looks but Mark finds her cute and funny. At least right up till the moment she stops being cute and funny.

"I'm never bored in your company," he often tells her.

She is bored in *his* company. Her theory is that being handsome since he was a tiny baby meant he had plenty of attention without having to develop a personality. Yes, he can be kind and easy-going but, thinking about it, she almost prefers Donna. Donna never makes her want to close her eyes and sleep for twenty-four hours.

Mondays are quiet at INFO-PULSE. Donna and Julie tend to chat a bit more although, as office manager, Donna is allowed to chat with her cowboy boots up on the desk while Julie has to pretend to work.

Suddenly, out of the blue, this particular Monday, Donna says, "I think it's so unfair at Christmas that members of staff who are part of a heterosexual couple get an extra afternoon off to go Christmas shopping. What do you think?"

As one half of a heterosexual couple, Julie is pleased to find out that she gets an extra afternoon off for Christmas shopping, but as it is only the beginning of July, she doesn't pay that much attention. She shrugs.

"So, you don't have an opinion? Why am I not surprised?" Donna turns towards the window as if addressing a crowd of people equally unsurprised by Julie's response.

"Couples," Julie does that inverted commas thing in the air each side of her head, "often have more presents to buy, what with in-laws and extended families to consider." She hopes that Donna will be impressed by her reference to 'extended families'.

"What about the lesbian and gay staff?" Donna asks.

"What about them?"

"The rights of lesbian and gay workers who are in a relationship should be considered as well."

"Oh, I agree."

Donna looks astonished. "You do?" Then she says, "Do you actually know anyone who is lesbian or gay?"

Quick as a flash Julie comes back with, "No, but I know a man who does."

Donna doesn't smile. She says, "What's that supposed to mean?"

"Nothing really. I was lightening the conversation. After all, it's hardly relevant, is it? I've lived for a quarter of a century and never met a single gay person."

"I'm a lesbian." Donna says this so casually, Julie thinks she could easily have been saying, "I'm a Somalian."

"So now what's your opinion on lesbian and gay staff in a relationship getting time off for Christmas shopping?"

Julie thinks about it. "Yes, they should," she says finally.

"Thank you."

"So, are you in a relationship then?" Julie asks, although she can't imagine anyone, male or female, wanting to spend entire days and nights with Donna.

"Not at the moment." Donna swings her boots off the desk and switches on her electric typewriter.

Julie concentrates on her work, filing Donna being a lesbian away to think about later on the bus home. She enjoys typing. It allows her time to daydream. She spends hours working out clothing combinations she'd look great in, right down to the last accessory and choice of signature colour. She glances across at Donna, who is wearing a floral-patterned shirt made from some unbreathable fabric like polyester, that does her no favours at all.

"Top Shop has some really stylish shirts," she says.

Donna doesn't look up but says, "Can I stop you there, Julie? This conversation is of no interest to me whatsoever."

Julie presses on, "Perhaps one lunchtime you and I could go shopping? I'm terrific at putting a look together."

"No thank you." Donna's voice is sort of strangled as if she is trying not to laugh.

Julie chooses to take this as a positive sign. "But Donna, it would be fun. I'd never force you into buying something you didn't like."

"Sorry, but you're the last person I'd choose to go shopping with."

"Why?"

Donna picks up her coffee mug and finds it empty. "Because only brainless ninnies with nothing much between their ears dress like you."

This is a strange moment. The two women stare across about six feet of space at each other. Julie's eyes register shock as if she's been landed a blow.

"Yes, you're right," she says quietly. "I would be brainless if there was nothing much between my ears."

"I'm sorry," Donna says. "That was rude of me."

"Yes, it was," Julie agrees. "I'll get coffee. Want some?"

"No, but thank you for asking."

Julie can't believe that Mark is still annoyed about his mum's wretched fruit trifle. Arriving home from work he goes straight upstairs to change without kissing the top of her head – which under normal circumstances would have been a relief, but in this instance means there'll be an atmosphere all evening, when she's gone to the trouble of cooking his favourite chicken Maryland pieces with potato wedges.

"You were right," she chirrups brightly, putting his plate in front of him.

"About what?" He skewers two potato wedges with his fork and sticks them into his mouth in a sort of angry, brutal manner.

"Donna from work is a lezzer."

His eyes are glacial. "And how does *she* feel about shop-bought trifle?"

Mark can keep an atmosphere going for weeks at a time. She has no option. Julie lowers her head, looks up at him through her eyelashes and says in the silly voice that she knows he loves, "I'm so vewy vewy sowee. I didn't mean to be howid about your mum's fruit trifle. Will Marky forgive his Julie?"

That does it. It always does do it. The chicken Maryland pieces sit congealing on the table while they heal their rift upstairs. During and afterwards, she wishes they hadn't, but then she thinks, *If I get it over with today, I may not have to do it again tomorrow.*

"I'm glad we're friends again," Mark says, pulling his jeans back on. "I know there's not an unkind bone in your gorgeous body."

He reaches out to tuck a strand of hair behind her ear, which immediately makes her want to embed her teeth into his hand. Instead she says brightly, "There's mandarin cheesecake and half-fat crème fraîche for afters."

Sometimes when Julie thinks of them having to live together for possibly another fifty years and have sex several times a week for at least half that time, she feels quite desperate. She imagines a path leading into a desert... and it isn't a desert like you see in holiday brochures with a hotel, swimming pool and sun loungers.

*

In the days following Donna calling her a brainless ninny, they start to get along better. Julie imagines that Donna feels worse about the tiff than she does, but Julie is feeling bad about other stuff. In the space of a fortnight she's admitted to herself that she wouldn't mind if her husband had a fatal car accident, that she finds him sleep-inducing and she almost prefers the company of the awful Donna. Deep down and the most unsettling is knowing she is hiding behind that insertion of 'almost'. Her weekends are no longer such a highlight; instead she looks forward to Mondays and seeing Donna. She even looks forward to their disagreements, sensing a reluctant affection creeping in behind Donna's insults. Increasingly, she keeps quiet and lets Donna talk, even sometimes listening to what she has to say.

One morning, Donna arrives at work in a particularly buoyant mood. When she goes to the cafeteria for her cappuccino, she brings one back for Julie, which she's never done before.

"Present." She lays a Bounty Bar next to Julie's coffee mug. "Guess what?"

"I'm no good at guessing, but thanks for the coffee and the chocolate."

"I'm going to America."

"Lucky you." Julie tries to sound genuinely enthusiastic, although America would never be her first choice of holiday destination... or even her fortieth. "How long for?"

"Maybe forever."

"You're taking your whole holiday allowance at once?"

"I'm giving in my notice."

Julie concentrates her gaze on the keyboard, before saying carelessly, "But you're in line for promotion. How will you manage without a job?"

"I've got savings. Eventually I'll get work in New York."

Julie wants to ask, *But Donna, won't you miss me?* Instead, again carelessly, she says, "Won't that be just a case of same work, different place?"

"Sometimes you can be quite insightful, Julie." Donna smiles at her. "You may even be right, but if I stay in this rut, nothing good will ever happen to me except that I might lose the will to live and end up conforming."

"And you'd hate that?"

"I would."

That evening Julie makes lasagne for Mark. He says it is delicious and reaches out to tuck a strand of hair behind her ear.

She says, "Mark, why do you keep pushing my hair behind my ears?"

"Do I, babe?"

"I think you do."

"I just love to touch you." His hand moves down to cup her chin.

What can she say? She's allowed seven years of Mark adjusting her hair to pass by without comment.

"I'll start stacking the dishwasher." Julie gets to her feet.

"Leave the dishes. Keep me company."

"I'll only be a minute."

From the kitchen, Julie heads out into the garden and sits on the bench. Ziggy joins her. It is dusk, quite chilly. She wraps her arms around the dog's neck. Ziggy makes a sound, a cross between a yawn and a yap of approval. Tiny black bats flit above their heads, silhouettes against the dark blue sky. She tries to lighten her mood. She isn't the type to feel sorry for herself. Julie actually despises people who bang on about feeling poorly or tired or what a miserable life they've had. When someone asks, "Why me?" she wants to answer, "Why not you?"

Mark opens one of the patio doors. "Julie, you'll catch cold out there."

"Just coming." She doesn't move.

Donna gives a month's notice. Each morning she ticks the day off on her 'Support a Pony Sanctuary' calendar. Julie is sick of the sight of two Shetland ponies staring at her reproachfully over a wooden fence.

"Julie, you can have this calendar when I go." Donna's voice is cheerful – a new norm for her.

Julie doesn't want the calendar. It is a poor substitute. "I'm not much of a calendar person."

"What sort of a person would that be?" Donna enquires, quirking an eyebrow at her.

Julie grins. "Someone who likes calendars."

"You're full of shit."

"I expect you're right," she says meekly.

Donna stands in front of Julie's desk, hands on her hips, expression baffled. "Why has it taken me all this time to find you fairly stimulating company?"

"Thanks," Julie says, dryly.

"I mean it. You're not my sort of person, but surprisingly you're quite likeable."

At this point Julie leaves her desk and heads for the ladies' toilet, where she washes her hands, taking ages to dry them on a paper towel. Then she walks out of the building and into the small park across the road, then twice around the War Memorial before returning to the office. Donna is slipping on her denim jacket.

"I'm off to lunch," she says cheerfully. "You all right?"

"Never better."

Donna hesitates. "I am sorry."

"What for?"

"For everything I say to you sounding so insulting."

Julie bends down under the desk and switches her electric typewriter on at the socket. "That's okay."

The door swings shut behind Donna. Julie hears the heels of her cowboy boots tapping smartly away down the corridor. She sits with her hands resting on the keyboard staring at Donna's empty chair and feeling confused. And worried. What is going on? Where has happiness gone?

She doesn't know whether she wants to take Mark to Donna's leaving party. The old Julie would have been keen to show her husband off to the rest of the staff because he is very good looking – but she doesn't want Donna seeing her as Mark's wife. The problem is that Julie isn't used to going out socially on her own. Mark's never encouraged friendships outside their family circle and, apart from Donna, she hasn't really made any friends at INFO-PULSE.

At her six-monthly appraisal, Donna had raised the subject of her inability to interact with other members of staff. "Julie," she said, "it is a disability in a company this size."

Julie hadn't thought of it as a 'disability', more a personal choice to keep herself to herself. She said, "My mother said friendships with boys would lead to teenage pregnancies and friendships with girls were unhealthy."

"Right." Donna nodded. "But supposing your husband went off with someone else?"

"He never would."

"But if he did, or something happened to him and you were left alone. How would you feel?"

She thought carefully before answering. Something happening to Mark? No more Mark? "Relieved," she said.

Donna dropped her pen. "Wouldn't you be devastated?"

"No. Not really." Simultaneously they grinned at each other and then they started laughing.

Mark sees Donna's leaving party as a big deal. He wants them to make an impressive entrance by co-ordinating his new suit worn with a salmon-pink tie with the salmon-pink sheath dress Julie bought for his mum and dad's coral wedding anniversary.

They both take the afternoon of the party off from work to get ready. "Mark, we're going to look stupid," Julie says, buckling the ankle straps on her four-inch-high silver stiletto-heeled shoes.

"Julie, we'll look fantastic – trust me."

They do look fantastic. They *also* look jaw-droppingly stupid. Julie actually sees jaws drop when they walk into the cafeteria looking like a third-division footballer and his wife. She remembers how, months ago, she wanted to see jaws drop at her school reunion. Nobody else has dressed up. Donna wears the same checked shirt and jeans she wore that morning.

Expression unreadable, Donna comes over. "Ah, the infamous Mark. Great to meet you at long last."

They shake hands.

Donna stares at Julie's dress, at her shoes. "Are you going on somewhere posh?"

"Yes," she says quickly. "We're eating at Bella Italia next to the cinema." It is the only restaurant she can think of.

Mark looks amazed. "But we've already had our dinner," he says.

"We've had a *snack*, Mark, but we're going on for dinner.

Let's get a drink. See you in a minute, Donna." Julie takes his elbow and pushes him towards the drinks table. "I'd like a dry white wine."

"But you always have apple juice."

Through gritted teeth she says, "Not today, I don't."

Everyone is staring at them. From the far side of the room, Donna mouths at her, "Are you okay?"

Julie feels incapable of even nodding or shaking her head. At that moment she hates Mark and all the staring strangers whose names she's never bothered to learn in the six months she's worked there. She reaches a decision: "Mark, I want to go. Now!"

"What about your dry white wine?"

Ignoring him, she almost runs towards the door, her movements clumsy in the tight dress and high heels.

"Julie, whatever's the matter?" Donna grabs her arm.

"Nothing. We've got to get to Bella Italia. We'll lose our table."

"You're making it up."

They stare at each other.

"What's the rush?" Mark asks. In one hand he holds a can of lager.

Julie turns her back on him.

"Calm down," Donna says gently. "It's okay."

But 'it' – whatever *it* is – is not okay. At any moment Mark will be shunting her through the door.

"Donna, I will *really* miss you," she blurts out.

In a low voice, Donna says, "I'll miss you too, darling."

Darling – that one word, so unlooked for, is a blade in Julie's heart.

Mark grips her by the shoulders. "Better get you home, babe. I think we'll skip the Italian restaurant."

*

Mark's mum has made a sherry trifle. It is horrible. Even Mark has difficulty pretending it is delicious but, because he loves his mum, he insists on a second helping.

"A little more for you, Julie?" His mum holds out a serving spoon of runny custard.

"Would love to, Mum, but I'm watching my waistline."

"I'm watching it as well." Mark winks at her.

In the lull before his mum begins to clear the table, Mark tells them about Donna's leaving party. "We were only there five minutes before Julie felt ill."

His dad asks, "Has this Donna got a husband or is she a divorcee?"

Mark flushes. "She's a lesbian, Dad."

"A what?"

"A lesbian."

Mark's dad studies his reflection in the smeared back of his dessert spoon before looking sternly across at Julie. "I hope she hasn't tried any funny stuff on with you?"

"No, Dad," she answers, knowing she should be offended at his tone of voice but suddenly feeling… apprehensive.

"Are you sure?"

"Did you say a lesbian?" Mark's mum pipes up.

"Not a word to bandy about at the dinner table." Mark's dad turns his attention to his son. "You want to keep an eye on your wife. Next thing you know she'll be joining the gay libbers."

"I don't think so, Dad." In vain Mark searches for Julie's hand under the table.

Gently, his mum changes the subject. "Mark, have you thought any more about going to the Motor Show in the autumn? Your dad's thinking about buying a Skoda. He's picked up some brochures."

Mark and his dad take the brochures into the lounge. Mark's mum begins to stack the plates. Not for the first time, Julie thinks she has a nice face, kind and sympathetic. Years ago, before she put on weight, Mark's mum would have been attractive. In a good way, she makes Julie think of a well-stuffed pillow in an apron.

"Any little ones on the horizon?" Mark's mum asks, and immediately Julie decides that likening her to a well-stuffed pillow in an apron is far too generous.

"Nope," Julie says.

"You're not getting any younger, dear."

"I'm only twenty-five."

"Twenty-six next birthday. We'd love a baby in the family."

Julie pushes back her chair. "Then *you* have it."

Julie goes out into the back garden. It has always seemed reassuringly old-fashioned, a meticulous rectangle of lawn bordered by flower beds of salvia, French marigolds and dahlias. There is a patio with two stone planters positioned each side of the patio doors, containing more salvia. Everything is neat and tidy. Visitors are discouraged from walking on the lawn, which is why Mark and Julie never bring their dog. Today the garden doesn't seem reassuring; it brings to the surface anxieties Julie has never ever been aware of, apart from perhaps at night when Mark has finally fallen asleep. Mark's father's garden represents her life: colourful, yes, but unexciting, unchanging and circumscribed.

She shivers. From behind her, through the open kitchen window, Mark's mum asks, "Are you all right, dear?"

Julie turns. "Time of the month, Mum. Sorry I was rude to you earlier."

That evening, while Mark is downstairs watching the television, she stands at the bedroom window, staring out at the night sky. Tomorrow there will be no Donna, no denim jacket hanging on the back of her chair, no click of cowboy boots.

"If anyone or anything is out there listening, I need a sign," she whispers.

The sign takes several weeks to arrive: a postcard of the Empire State Building. On the back Donna has written, "Considering we had so little in common, I find I'm missing your daily load of bollocks. Write if you want," then an address.

Over Julie's shoulder, Mark reads the postcard. "I hope you're not thinking of writing back," he says. "I'd stick that straight in the dustbin."

She doesn't answer.

He raises a hand to tuck away that recalcitrant strand of hair.

"Don't!"

Mark hesitates and then with a sort of snigger in his voice, says, "Come on, Julie. Surely, you're not falling for this woman, are you?"

Julie shakes her head.

Their eyes meet.

"Not yet," she says.

Mark's hand falters and falls.

Part 2

Julie is now recording all her private thoughts in a diary. Not for one moment does she think that Mark will ever read it. For a start he has never shown an interest in reading anything apart from car brochures and super-hero comics. And then again, because *she* has little curiosity about other people or what makes them tick, she assumes the same disinterest from him. Somewhere Julie has heard the phrase 'hidden in plain sight', so the small, leather-bound book lies amongst her fashion magazines and regular subscription for *House Beautiful* on the hall table. When she's not fashioning an imaginary, clandestine love affair with Donna, she muses on how brilliant it would be if her diary entries were snapped up by a publisher and turned into a best-selling novel that within days of publication raced up the romantic fiction charts – but romantic fiction with a twist. *Julie Norman – a laugh and a tear on every page!*

None of this light-hearted stuff means that Julie is happy. On the contrary.

"I ricochet between excitement, euphoria and fear," she writes. "I'm seeing a three-sided room with steel walls and one bullet – me – on a painful and bewildering trajectory." And in the days following the arrival of Donna's postcard: "The heart is a complicated and capricious organ." Although not her own words, they perfectly suit her emotional state. Inexplicably, having yearned to renounce her marriage and fly to Donna's side, she is now more cautious. Julie yearns for change, possibly even romance, but the reality of putting her marriage in jeopardy is a frightening one and to be avoided at all costs.

While Julie dithers around what response she should make, if any, she discovers that Donna is back in London.

It is a Tuesday morning. Julie is in the canteen queue waiting to order a pot of Earl Grey tea and a Bounty Bar. She doesn't particularly like Bounty Bars but they now hold a romantic significance. In front of her stand two women whom she recognises, although even after almost a year at INFO-PULSE Julie still has no idea what their names are.

Woman 1: "I heard Donna the Dyke's asked for her old job back but Pretty-in-Pink's managing perfectly well without her. With PP, Frank only has to pay her the junior typist's rate."

(Frank is one of the company directors and considered something of a creep by all the staff apart from Julie, who likes him because she thinks he likes her.)

Woman 2: "Frank's just waiting to climb into Pretty-in-Pink's knickers at the Christmas party."

They both smirk.

Julie taps Woman 2 on the shoulder.

The woman turns her head, looks startled and then embarrassed.

"Excuse me, nobody's climbing into *my* knickers," Julie says sweetly. "And actually, I look pretty whatever colour I'm wearing!" She dumps her tray on the counter and leaves the two of them with their mouths hanging open.

The next day at work, Donna rings. Just hearing Donna's voice makes Julie feel as if her heart is lodged in her throat, which initially makes conversation impossible. She produces the sound a frog might make.

"Brid-ip."

"Julie, are you there?" Donna asks.

"Brid-ip."

"Have you got a cold?"

"Not really."

"Well, you've either got a cold or you haven't." Donna sounds irritated.

"Air pollution," Julie answers. But then, before she can stop herself, she blurts out, "Oh Donna, I have missed you."

"I've only been gone a matter of weeks."

What has happened to the intense woman who called her 'darling'?

They both start talking at the same time.

"Perhaps we could meet up?" Julie says.

"Actually, I've missed you too," from Donna.

They laugh – although it is embarrassed laughter – and agree to meet up in five days' time at Angel tube station.

"Look forward to it," Julie says.

"Yeah," from Donna.

Two days beforehand, Julie realises that in equal measures she can't wait to see Donna and is dreading seeing Donna – this will be the first-ever step she's taken outside the boundary of her marriage. Since her ambiguity over the postcard, she and Mark are hardly on speaking terms, but he still represents the safe, comforting and even preferable option. Call Julie superficial, but her dream of an affair with a woman who's moved to the other side of the world suddenly becomes less appealing when the love-interest lives just forty-five minutes away by train.

Donna is a lesbian and Julie knows nothing much about

lesbians except that they sleep with other lesbians. Supposing, when they meet, their relationship changes in a heartbeat from one of banter and affection to a declaration of love, or an expectation of love and sex? Julie ending up in bed with Donna? That has never been part of her daydreams... with anyone!

One day to go and Donna telephones. "It won't be just the two of us. I thought I'd introduce you to a few of my friends. See how you all get along. Jan and Rosie have a garden flat in Islington."

Julie is relieved, yet disappointed.

Date night! Julie has arranged to leave work mid-afternoon so she can catch a train into London. She tells Mark that INFO-PULSE is stock-taking so she won't be home till after nine. She always carries a roomy shoulder bag for her makeup and perfume spray, but this particular day she adds – carefully folded so they won't crease – a thin summer skirt and blouse, silver sandals and a matching slimline clutch bag. The skirt and blouse are new, bought in the lunch hour and never shown to Mark. They are oh, so pretty; made of white cotton voile and decorated with a pattern of strawberries. In INFO-PULSE's toilet mirror, her reflection looks... well, wonderful. Her eyes shine. Everything about Julie shines.

As she walks through the general office, Frank wolf-whistles. "Looking good, Julie," he calls out.

"Why thank you, kind sir." She makes a half-curtsey, and off she goes, out into the sunshine.

She's been to Islington before. It has great shops and elegant houses. She imagines a gathering of equally elegant women who – if Frank's reaction to her is anything to go by – will be impressed with the beauty that is... Julie. Conveniently, she blots out all the criticisms Donna has levelled at her clothes, thoughts and marriage status in the past. If anything, she has transformed them into a form of flirtation, when you insult a beloved one to attract their attention.

At Angel Station, Julie spots Donna first. She's standing at the ticket barrier reading a copy of the *Evening Standard*. She's lost weight *and* her pink highlights. In all the time they worked together, Julie never once found Donna physically attractive, but now she does.

"Donna," she calls out, almost running the last few steps.

Donna looks up, her face impassive. "Hi Julie."

Julie sort of half-pirouettes in front of her. "Pleased to see me?"

Donna hesitates. "Of course."

They leave the station, Donna tossing the paper into a bin as they walk towards the traffic lights. Julie wonders if she'll take her hand, but no she doesn't. Once again, Julie is relieved and yet disappointed.

The lights turn green and they cross the road. Ahead of them, their images are reflected in a store window. Julie frowns. They look completely mismatched, just two random women from very different lives and backgrounds who, on reaching the pavement, will turn away and walk off in different directions. But never mind being mismatched with Donna, Julie is mismatched with Islington. She has dressed for a garden party or afternoon tea at a vicarage somewhere in the countryside. Julia glances anxiously at Donna, who is also mesmerised by their reflection – and not in a good way.

"I'm sorry if I've worn the wrong clothes," Julie says.

Donna shrugs. "You're fine."

A sheet of ice has fallen between them. Julie actually shivers. Silently they walk for about ten minutes. In her flimsy sandals, Julie struggles to keep up. In the past she has resented the way Mark insists on shepherding her across roads and through crowds, opens doors for her and reaches proprietorially for her hand. Suddenly it would be a relief to be walking hand in hand with *him* rather than this stranger.

They turn into a less crowded residential street. On each side are tall Victorian houses, most of them with long untidy front gardens.

Donna reaches for her hand. "I'm sorry," she says. "This must seem so weird."

"A bit." Julie has never held hands with a woman before. Supposing they bump into someone she knows, someone from work, one of Mark's relations – what will they think?

"Here we are." Donna pushes open a gate.

There is a path of broken paving stones and several overflowing dustbins. On the front step a woman wearing drab grey clothes with drab grey hair is waiting. Donna lets go of Julie's hand.

"Welcome home, sunshine." The woman puts her arms around Donna's waist and kisses her directly on the mouth.

Julie finds the casual intimacy somehow shocking.

"Glad to be back?" the woman asks Donna.

"Never thought I'd say this, Jan, but yes I am."

The woman looks over her shoulder. "And you are?"

"Julie."

"Julie?" Jan raises her eyebrows. "Come on in."

Julie follows them into the narrow hall and down to a large untidy kitchen. Several women sit on two long benches at a wooden table littered with plates and bottles. They are drinking wine. Another woman stands on the step of the open patio doorway smoking a cigarette. On the cluttered worktop, in a patch of late sunshine, two cats sleep. Julie is ignored as everyone greets Donna like the return of the prodigal daughter. Reluctantly it seems, Donna half-turns towards her. "And this is Julie."

The kitchen falls silent. The women scrutinise her. In their faces Julie reads curiosity and mistrust. She belongs to an alien species: the straight married woman species. A dabbler. Not to be taken seriously.

"Bloody hell!" The woman standing in the doorway tosses her cigarette out into the garden and steps back into the kitchen. "I say, anyone for Ascot?"

Nobody laughs. Donna says nothing but looks uncomfortable.

Jan steps forward. "Rosie, that's enough. Have some manners."

"But Jan, sweetheart..." Rosie spreads out her hands and grins at her audience. "It's even carrying a clutch bag."

Jan turns to Julie and says quite kindly, "Take no notice. Tea, coffee, wine?"

Everyone is drinking wine, but Mark will smell it on Julie's breath. If she asks for tea or coffee, these women will despise her. "A glass of tap water, please."

Rosie snorts.

The evening is not a success. Julie is out of her depth. She has no idea how to reach Donna's friends – or Donna for that matter. After an hour of being ignored, of Donna avoiding meeting her gaze, she slips away. In the toilet at Euston Station she changes back into the clothes she wore to work. She dumps the pretty skirt and blouse, the uncomfortable sandals, in a waste bin. Mark has asked her to ring from the phone booth near the bus shelter and he'll collect her in the car. She doesn't ring. She walks the half-mile home.

"Why didn't you ring?" Mark asks.

"There was a queue."

He looks at her as if he doesn't believe her.

Months pass. Donna hasn't given her an address or telephone number but even if she had, Julie wouldn't get in touch. She has some pride left. She feels horribly hurt. At first, she assumes the pain will fade, but each morning there it is – a powerful and dark cloud in her heart. Constantly she goes over the way Donna's friends treated her, while Donna – with all her ideals and support of good causes – didn't say a word in her defence.

Finally, at work, a letter is handed in for her. Frank calls out, "From a secret admirer?"

Julie smiles stiffly. "I don't think so." She drops the envelope into her bag. At lunchtime she walks across to the walled garden in nearby Gadebridge Park. Sitting on a bench, she opens the envelope and finds a brief note with no address or phone number.

"Julie – so sorry I let you down. I apologise for my friends but they worry about me getting involved with a married woman and you really are very much a married woman. Be happy with Mark."

She scrutinises Donna's words for something personal apart from "you really are very much a married woman". Surely Donna had seen that from the start. Why send that postcard from America? Why arrange the meeting? When she arrives home that evening she tucks the note into the back of her diary.

Julie has hit rock bottom, or that is how it feels. As if she's been chucked out of an aeroplane and landed badly... as you would if chucked out of an aeroplane. But as weeks become months, she's horrified at how close she came to throwing away Mark, his family, her status – all on an infatuated whim.

As she explains to Ziggy on one of their evening walks around the block, "No way would I give up a three-bedroomed house, garden, car, clothes, holidays, even Mark's mum's Sunday dinners, to live in a shabby flat in London and wear dungarees and have my hair cut short like Mark's dad wears his!"

Ziggy looks back over his shoulder at her and pants adoringly.

"No way could I give you up either, darling."

Julie has come to her senses. Surely danger has been averted! Or has it? The one thing Julie finds she can't – repeat, *can't* – do, is face sex with Mark. No more fluttering her eyelashes, no silly voice or acquiescent droop of her head; instead she weaves and dives and claims the longest periods in history. Julie can't bear Mark to even touch her. The strain on both of them is devastating.

One evening over dinner, Mark asks, apparently casually, "So Julie, do you not want sex anymore because you'd rather do it with your friend Donna?"

She chokes on a mouthful of chicken and leek pie. "Don't be stupid," she says. "Donna's in America."

He looks at her, his eyes cold. "No, she isn't. I saw her at the NEC when I went with Dad to the Motor Show. She was there with a couple of lezzers."

"But the Motor Show was weeks ago. Why didn't you tell me?"

"I was waiting for *you* to tell me."

"I had no idea." She concentrates on cutting a perfect square of pastry. "I'm surprised she hasn't kept in touch."

"Julie, you don't fool me for a minute."

"Mark, I'm not lying."

He pushes back his chair and gets to his feet. "If you are seeing her, she's obviously not making you happy. You look bloody awful."

The comment about her looks knocks the wind out of Julie. He sees it in her face and for a moment his eyes soften.

She lays down her knife and fork and looks up at him. "I'm not seeing Donna. I promise you."

He places his hands on the table and leans quite menacingly towards her. "Then why don't you want sex?"

She tells him she hasn't felt well. She agrees to see the doctor and try harder. That night she does try, but whereas in the past Mark has never seemed to notice her lack of enthusiasm, this time he does. Unsatisfied, he rolls off her and lies with his arm behind his head staring up at the ceiling. Julie pretends to fall asleep. An hour later he gently pushes back the duvet and goes into the spare room.

For Mark's birthday, as always, she books The Wild Goose, their local Harvester. This year there will only be Mark's parents, his brother David and David's wife Alice. Mark's sister and her husband are on a Fred Olsen cruise ship sailing into the heart of the Norwegian fjords.

Julie knows The Wild Goose better than she knows the back of her hand. She and Mark have been going there for family celebrations for years. If the weather's bad, they invariably sit inside by the window, overlooking the car park; if good, at the table and benches outside next to the fire pit. Mark's dad buys all the drinks. He and his sons enjoy pints and male conversation at the bar for half-hours at a time between courses.

Mark and Julie are the first to arrive. It has been a strange and uncomfortable day, with Mark accepting the presents

Oh You Pretty Thing

she has bought for him almost with suspicion.

It is November and the weather has turned cold so they sit inside, in silence, staring out across the car park. In happier times they would have chattered easily to each other, exchanging enjoyable trivialities.

"Oh, there's David," Julie exclaims – and then, just for the sake of approaching a proper conversation, "Do you think he regrets selling his motorbike?"

"I'm sure he does but he has responsibilities now." Mark gets to his feet to greet his brother and sister-in-law. "In a few months' time he'll be a daddy," he says. There is absolutely no warmth in his voice.

Same people, same venue, same conversations, but not quite. Even though it's Mark's birthday, the focus today is on Alice, Mark's pregnant sister-in-law.

Julie watches Mark cross the car park towards their car. His smile of greeting is forced. David helps Alice out of the car, then turns to his brother and squeezes his arm. Leisurely, the three of them walk towards the pub. Julie waves. Only Alice waves back. Mark's parents' car pulls in. Nobody seems to be in any hurry to join Julie at the table.

She makes a note on a paper napkin to transfer into her diary later on. "Hate the lot of them. Donna would hate them too. How will I get through the rest of my life?"

Actually, Julie quite likes Alice. In the past at these family gatherings, Alice has been her ally. They share a love of clothes, a love of colour. They've even enjoyed a shopping trip together. But Mark didn't like the idea, said afterwards, "I'm not sure about Alice. She has rather too much to say for herself."

Normally on these occasions, Mark drapes his arm along the back of the banquette behind Julie's head, his hand stroking her shoulder, neck, ear, hair; but today they sit stiffly with six inches of space between them, staring straight ahead. Julie imagines their changed behaviour goes unobserved, but of course it doesn't.

Mark's father leans across the table towards her. "And when are *you* going to give me a grandchild?"

"Better ask Mark," Julie says.

"I'm asking you." There is hostility in his voice.

"I can't give you an answer."

Mark's dad gives her a long cold stare before turning to Alice. "Come up with any names for the sprog?"

Alice grins, a wide pink grin showing bright pink gums. "If it's a boy, we'll call him Mark. If it's a girl we'll call her Cherry after Julie."

Mark's dad laughs loudly and raises his beer glass. "Here's hoping the baby's a boy!"

Julie calls down the table to Alice, "Why not Julie?"

Alice says, "We all think of you as a cherry. A bright pink cherry."

Mark's mother looks embarrassed. "Sorry Julie. I told them how you reminded me of a pink cherry. It was a compliment. We all like pink cherries, don't we?"

Everyone nods, except Mark. He pushes his plate away.

"Mark, you've hardly eaten anything," Julie says.

He ignores her. "Drink before pudding, Dad?"

His dad and brother throw their napkins down on the table and head for the bar, leaving Julie with Alice and her mother-in-law. At first no one speaks. Finally, Alice says, "So, what's up with you and Mark?"

"Nothing." Julie shrugs and smiles.

"Close your ears, Mum," Alice says, then turns back to Julie. "Mark told my David that you two haven't had sex in months."

"Alice!" Mark's mother looks horrified.

Alice laughs. "Well, I told you not to listen. Come on, Julie, spill the beans."

Julie's head, face, entire body feels as if it is blushing with shame. She is so unprepared. Weakly she answers, "Mark shouldn't be talking about our personal life with other people."

"Well, he has to talk to someone." Alice moves into Mark's seat. "Mark said you're having an affair with a woman."

Mark's mother says, "Alice, you're going to ruin the evening and we haven't cut the cake or sung 'Happy Birthday' yet."

Alice turns back to Julie and whispers, "You're not really a lesbian, are you?"

Julie thinks, *I am a Julie; one half of an attractive young couple.* She takes a deep breath as if making ready to fight for her life. "Alice, please be careful about spreading lies about me." Her tone is icy.

"Well, if the cap fits."

"And what cap would that be?" The heightened colour is fading from Julie's cheeks and she feels totally calm.

"You and another woman."

At the bar, the men have almost finished their drinks. Any moment now they will be returning to the table. Julie settles herself against the padded back of the banquette and says very slowly, as if she is unconcerned and has all the time in the world, "Actually, Alice, I don't even like women – and that includes you." She picks up the wine bottle. There are only a few inches of wine left in it. Julie empties it into her glass. "If I did have an affair, it would definitely be with a man."

"Now that's enough of that sort of talk," Mark's mum snaps.

David has peeled off to go to the gents', but Mark and his father are nearing the table. Julie narrows her eyes and focuses on Alice. "But I'm not having an affair. Mark and I are very much in love and I won't let any of you –" she switches her gaze to her mother-in-law – "put our marriage in jeopardy with your female gossip."

Mark and his dad reach the table. Julie fills her eyes with tears. She stumbles to her feet – her bread knife and side plate dropping to the wooden floor. The plate breaks.

"Julie!" Mark says.

With one hand she brushes the tears away and tries to push past him.

He holds her by the elbow. "Sweetheart, whatever's the matter?"

Tears stream down her face. "Perhaps you'd better ask Alice," she sobs. "I'm going outside for a breath of fresh air."

Ten minutes later he joins her in the pub garden, his expression lighter than it has been in weeks. "They've all gone home. There's been an almighty row. I'm so sorry."

"How could they think that of me? How could you think that of me? And to talk to your family behind my back. To gang up on me."

He looks uncomfortable. "The postcard started it. You said you were writing back. Then seeing that woman at the Motor Show... and you've been so distant."

Julie cuts in, "I was angry and upset that you could even think such things about me. Yes, I liked Donna, but as a friend. You have your dad and your brother. Sometimes I want another woman to talk to. That doesn't make me a lesbian, does it?" She ends on another sob.

"Oh Julie, babe." He tries to take her hands. "Of course you're not a lesbian."

"How could you be so disloyal? After all these years surely *I* should have been the person to talk to if you had doubts?"

It is easy to confuse Mark, to make him think all of this is just a misunderstanding fuelled by his jealous imagination. It is only later that night in bed, wrapped in each other's arms, as they celebrate his birthday and their reconciliation, that Julie's thoughts turn to Donna and then to Donna's note, the words that she knows by heart: *You really are very much a married woman.*

Part 3

The weather is only so-so, but that's okay with Mark. Had the sun shone, he'd have been worrying that Julie would rather be in the garden on a sun lounger than accompanying him to B&Q with the promise of a meal later at a country pub.

On the surface, the two of them are getting along much better, but it's at night, in bed, where the problems surface.

Unbeknown to Julie, Mark is still confiding in his brother, David. *His* advice has been to redecorate their bedroom. "Julie will love it," David enthuses. "Get her involved. The two of you sit down one evening with a glass of wine and bond over those *House Beautiful* magazines she used to pass on to Alice."

This almost works. Julie is happy to talk fabric and colour schemes. The night before, the two of them looking through the magazines together, Julie became quite enthusiastic, tearing out pictures of room settings, bed linen and paint shades. They drank a couple of glasses of wine each and made a list of products they needed to buy initially. Just at the end of the evening, when she actually began to look relaxed for the first time in months, he ruined it all. He was a little intoxicated, so pleased to see her happy.

"Come and sit on my lap, babe," Mark said, patting his knees.

"I'm quite happy on the sofa." Julie didn't look up from her magazine.

"Then I'll come and join you." He sat next to her, lifting up her legs and arranging them across his thighs. Immediately he felt her stiffen.

"Mark!" She tried to swing her legs off him. He held on and it became a struggle between them. "I'm not a Barbie Doll!" She almost screamed the words at him.

"But you are my wife!" he shouted back at her.

Julie stopped struggling. All the tension left her body. "Fair enough," she said, picking up the magazine again. "Now let me see, star signs."

He let a few moments pass, reached for his wine glass and emptied it. Then he began to stroke her ankles. When she didn't resist or say anything, his hands climbed higher to cup her knees

Julie slapped her magazine down hard across his knuckles. "That's enough!"

"It's not enough for me."

"I'm not your property to maul when and where you like!" She jumped to her feet, went to bed, leaving him to open another bottle of wine.

Going shopping, or on any outing, is no longer enjoyable for either of them. Getting ready to drive to B&Q, they are not good-naturedly vying for space in front of the full-length mirror. There is no affectionate banter. They've become cautious about what they say. Everything and anything is capable of opening up recent wounds. Julie gets dressed. Mark gets dressed. They avoid even glancing at each other. Mark leaves Julie to finish her makeup while he packs their shopping bags in the back of the car. Julie looks down from the bedroom window. Mark is leaning against the driver's door with his arms folded. He appears utterly miserable.

Cars are a big deal to Mark. His present choice is an Audi Quattro Coupé in silver grey, the deposit borrowed from his dad. It looks smart. In the past, they shared a pride in what their cars said about them, that they were young and successful. As she watches Mark, along with regret about the mess she's created she can't help thinking admiringly, *Mark and the car look like they're part of a classy tv advert.*

As she steps out onto the drive Mark is already holding the passenger door open for her. She smiles up at him as if everything is hunky-dory between them, just in case a neighbour might be looking out of *their* window. "Thank you darling," she says.

He smiles back, a little awkwardly.

"Mark! Julie!" A woman's voice cuts across this attractive domestic vignette. Julie recognises one of their neighbours from several houses away. The woman lives with her daughter. In happier days, Mark and Julie speculated on where the husband was. They decided he wasn't dead, he'd just got tired of her screeching voice and bleach-blonde hair. Julie has no idea of their names so it comes as a surprise to find that the woman knows theirs. Julie reminds herself that probably everyone in the road knows who they are because they look so remarkable: so much a prosperous, attractive young couple destined for a detached modern house with double garage on an exclusive estate. It's laughable really.

The woman is in her forties, figure not bad, but with one of those tanned, heavily lined faces that indicates a heavy smoker who holidays abroad and roasts herself under full sun while slapping on the minimum sun screen. Daughter, standing behind the line of straggling shrubs that hedge their front garden, is a younger version of mother but fatter.

"Morning Janet," Mark says cheerfully.

Julie is amazed. How does Mark know her name?

Without glancing in Julie's direction, Janet flip-flops on her flip-flops into their driveway and parks herself in front of Mark, her breasts grazing the zipper of his bomber jacket. "You're not going anywhere near B&Q, are you?"

He gives her a big friendly grin of the kind that Julie has observed men give to women they hardly know, yet are trying to impress. "Indeed, we are."

Julie chokes. She wants to lean out of the car window and shout, "Indeed, we aren't."

"Is there anything you'd like me to pick up for you, while we're there?" Mark asks.

"Actually," Janet tweaks the toggle of his zip – as if Julie isn't sitting only three feet away from them! "I wondered if me and Susie could blag a lift?"

Mark looks at his watch. "If you and Susie can be ready to go in the next five minutes, we'd be happy to give you a lift. Wouldn't we, Julie?"

Janet doesn't hang about for any approval from Julie. "Two minutes," she says and whisks out onto the pavement.

Mark gets in the car. "I know you're annoyed but what else could I do?"

"You could have said, 'I'm sorry Janet, but we're heading in the opposite direction.' You realise we'll be stuck with them for the rest of the day? They'll want a lift home as well."

"Well, I can hardly leave them marooned."

"There are buses."

"How the hell would you know?" He slaps the steering wheel with the palms of his hands. "For god's sake, Julie, don't start."

"*I'm* not starting anything. You're the one who has just ruined my Saturday."

He glares at her, his face filled with... she can't say anger, more frustration. And fair enough, she is being an uncharitable bitch. On the verge of apologising, she sees mother and daughter hurrying towards them. Susie is late teens, early twenties. Both wear sweatshirts and jeans. Janet has kept to her flip-flops while Susie's trainers are blindingly white. Absolutely no competition, as far as Julie is concerned. She also wears trainers, but these are expensive, palest rose pink with silver detail and laces.

Working on the premise, 'if you can't join them, patronise them,' Julie plays the part of gracious, enviable young wife; woman with the handsome husband, top-of-the-range new car, Everest double-glazing and a tasteful cherub water feature in her front garden. She is in control. But no, she's not. Far from it.

The twenty-minute car drive proves to be a nightmare. Janet and Susie never stop talking to Mark, while he metamorphoses from the Mark who idolises his precious Julie to a version of 'man in a bar' chatting up two women he finds attractive. It is like she's been married for eight years to a Jekyll and Hyde character. And what is even more bewildering, Mark seems to know them quite well. He asks after Susie's boyfriend, Neil. Covertly watching her in the rear-view mirror, Julie counts five good-sized pimples festering on Susie's two chins. How has Susie landed a boyfriend?

Mark asks after Janet's divorce. "I expect you're glad to see the back of him, Janet. A real waste of space if ever I saw one."

Each query from Mark elicits a storm of response. Janet never uses one word when twenty are available. She and her daughter shout, cackle, swear, make jokes that are *not* funny, with Mark providing the highly attentive audience. Even if Julie wanted to, she couldn't get a word in edgeways. For a few minutes while they are stuck at traffic lights she actually considers getting out of the car but she doubts they'd even notice her exit.

At B&Q the two factions split up. When Mark calls after them, "Give me a shout if you need any advice," she pinches his arm hard.

"That hurt!"

"Sorry Mark, but do you mind if we just enjoy ourselves *à deux* for half an hour?" Julie tries to smile light-heartedly, tries to be Mark's original, girlish Julie. "After all, what advice could *you* give them? Darling, you know nothing about DIY. Your dad dictates a list of products to buy and then he does most of the work."

Not very successful. Mark storms off in the direction of the paint aisle, leaving her feeling weary with herself, an ill-natured dot standing on her own in a cavernous warehouse, liked by nobody – not by Mark, their neighbours or Donna. What does it matter that she's part-owner of a car, house, garden, double-bloody-glazing?

Mark's distant figure turns. He shouts, "Are we looking for paint, or what?"

"Coming." She hurries to catch him up.

They stare at a paint chart. "What do you think?" Mark asks. Julie picks up the uncertainty in his voice and her irritation vanishes. Again, she just feels sorry. Sorry that she couldn't really care less what colour the bedroom walls are.

"You choose," she says.

"No, I want you to choose. Something pretty perhaps. What about Blossom Pink?"

Long afterwards, Julie will remember this moment because Mark's question triggers something, flicks a switch somewhere. In her head is the thought, *Let Mark have the colour he wants, because you won't be here much longer.*

"What colour do you really like, Mark?" Her tone of voice is serious. It surprises both of them.

He smiles sheepishly, "I quite like the French Grey."

"I like that one as well. Perhaps just brilliant white gloss for the woodwork?"

Paint bought, they sit in the car and wait. For both of them, it feels as if they've called a truce. Time passes. After forty minutes, Julie sends Mark back into the store to find Janet and Susie. "There'll be nothing left of our day, if they don't get a move on," she says.

Mark returns without them, grinning from the encounter. "Ten more minutes. They can't agree on lampshades – the daft pair."

Julie would like to ask, "Whoever would buy their lampshades from B&Q?" but doesn't. She does mutter, "If either of them suggests stopping somewhere for lunch, please say 'no'!"

Mark sighs. "You can be a real cow, Julie. Cut them some slack."

"Fair enough." Inside she feels so sad that once again she's destroying his good mood.

Finally, they see them dawdling across the car park. With one hand Janet pushes the trolley, in the other she holds a burger. Susie too carries a burger and a greasy paper bag.

"Mark," Janet screeches from some distance away. "We've bought you one as well."

He gets out of the car and opens the boot. "Thanks," he says. "Shopping's made me hungry." He loads their stuff into the car before taking the greasy bag from Susie.

Susie peers at Julie through the passenger window, a little shame-faced. "We didn't think you'd want one, Julie."

Oh You Pretty Thing

"You were right." She smiles sweetly up at Susie but nobody is fooled.

"They're scrummy," Janet says. Then to Mark, "How do you put up with your missus? She's a miserable bat, isn't she?"

Julie snaps, "Don't be so bloody rude."

"Oh, you've got a voice then – you hardly said a word on the way here." Janet laughs, opening her mouth, displaying the mixture of chewed grey meat and greasy onions.

Julie looks at Mark. "Can you finish that disgusting burger and take me home?"

"I'm not getting indigestion just to please you." Mark turns his back on her and continues eating. Between mouthfuls he starts up a conversation with Janet about lampshades.

Julie grabs her jacket and pushes open the car door. The two women watch her as she sets off towards the giant Tesco's.

Janet shouts, "Get me a pint of full-cream milk."

Julie walks slowly, each moment expecting Mark to either run after her or call out. She won't look back at them, instead she bypasses the store, taking the slope leading back to the main road. The shopping complex disappears behind the trees and hedgerow. The verge to her left is hip-high with grasses, fronds of cow parsley, and scarlet poppies. A few cars beep her. No sign of Mark, but suddenly she doesn't want Mark, and definitely not the hateful Janet and her daughter.

A rough path – little more than an animal track – leads away from the road and she takes it. The weather had been grey and dismal but now, as if to encourage her, the sun comes out, pleasantly warm on her back. Julie is so rarely on her own. She feels all the anger and resentment about *everything* begin to recede. The sense of quiet clothes her – or that is how it feels. She laughs uncertainly. And then she begins to run, not from fear, but because it seems necessary to be running.

She feels as if she could run for miles without pause, as if all there is in the world is the fresh green grass beneath her feet and the blue sky above her head – and that's enough. In the moment before Julie erupts out onto the hard shoulder, her face cracks into a smile at the feeling of absolute exhilaration. She is free.

But here at the roadside is Mark's car, the doors open and Mark leaning on the bonnet. Janet sprawls across the passenger seat, her legs stretched out onto the verge. She is smoking a cigarette, while Susie lies nearby, flat on the grass, jeans rolled up to her knees – presumably to catch the weak rays of sun.

Janet says, "We watched you running across that bit of field. You were visible from the road."

Julie's feelings change from euphoria to horror. She sees what they see: a panting mad woman, a wild animal they are patiently waiting to return to captivity.

Mark strides towards her. He looks furious. "What's the matter with you? Have you taken leave of your senses?"

Behind him, Susie sits up. She looks at her mum. Janet shrugs and mouths, "Gah-gah!"

"I'm sorry, Mark," Julie says meekly.

"*You're* sorry?" His hand firmly on her shoulder, he walks her back to the car. Julie imagines a police drama where the cops duck the prisoner's head down to guide them into the back of the Black Maria.

Janet throws her cigarette butt out into the road and gets to her feet. She stretches and moves away from the door so Julie can reclaim her seat. In silence they drive homewards. Finally, to relieve the tension in the car, Julie asks Janet, "Did you get the wallpaper you wanted?"

"Yes," Janet says. "And the lampshades."

*

Oh You Pretty Thing

There is a respite. The worst sort. On arriving home, as Mark unlocks the front door, the phone rings.

"Yes?" he snarls, and then his face softens. He glances at Julie as if for reassurance and immediately she reaches for his hand. His eyes fill with tears. "David, I am so sorry," he says.

Julie mouths, "What's happened?"

He shakes his head and turns away, listening intently. He says, "Ring when you're back. I'll come over."

Alice has lost the baby.

This is a serious, adult event in their lives. It draws them together, brings out the best in Julie and Mark. They have other people to think of rather than themselves. Julie visits Alice in the hospital but there is nothing she can find to say to help the listless woman in the bed. As she's about to leave, Alice says with anger in her voice, "I'm not a bloody Friesian cow."

Julie has no idea what she means but answers, "Of course you're not."

There is more to come. One morning, a month later, Alice sets off for work and doesn't come back. She leaves behind a forwarding address and a note.

"Dear David, I know how much you want children so I'm giving you the chance to have them with someone else. I'm heartbroken about the baby but I wasn't ready to settle down. Selling your motorbike and wanting to be a dad was the final straw for me."

Mark and David pore over this piece of paper for hours trying to make sense of it. Just once, at first, they show it to Julie. Then they keep it to themselves as if fearful that Julie will understand what Alice means and they won't like her interpretation.

During that time, Julie is probably as fond of Mark as she's ever been. Were he just an admiring neighbour, she could easily have spent a comfortable lifetime chatting over the fence, accepting lifts to the shops, walking the dog together and flirting mildly. He might still be a good friend, a best friend, but she can't live in the same house with Mark, the husband, although it takes a while longer to tell him that.

It is a sunny but cool Saturday and the family will be meeting that afternoon at The Wild Goose to celebrate Mark's father's retirement. Julie, wearing jeans and a plain blue shirt, is sprawled on the sofa looking through one of her magazines.

"Oh, put on something pretty," Mark says, carrying in a mug of tea from the kitchen.

She ignores him.

"Please Julie, let's not spoil the day."

Julie tosses the magazine aside and goes upstairs. She calls down, "Do I need a pullover?"

"Of course not. We'll be indoors and pullovers don't suit you."

Ten minutes later, Julie is back wearing the same jeans. She has changed her shirt for a ruffled blouse. "Will this do?"

Mark doesn't respond. He's sitting on the sofa with his back to her, his head bent over something. Next to him is a pile of her magazines. He seems unnaturally still.

"Are you okay?" she asks.

Mark doesn't answer or look up. He shuts her diary and places Donna's letter on top of it, then nudges both along the coffee table towards her. Quite conversationally he says, "So, all this time, you've been lying to me?"

She moistens her lips. "Not really," she says. "As is clear in the note, nothing happened between us."

"Not clear at all." He still hasn't looked at her. Instead he picks up the sheet of paper and reads out: "'I apologise for my friends but they worry about me getting involved with a married woman.' I particularly like the 'Be happy with Mark'. But you're not happy, are you?"

She feels as if she's been waiting for this question for years. Her eyes are apologetic. "I'm sorry, Mark, but no."

He reaches for the mug of tea. His hand shakes. Tea slops onto the coffee table.

Julie huddles in the armchair. "It was an infatuation. It's in the past. I met her once and nothing happened."

From the pocket of his jeans, Mark takes out a handkerchief and begins to wipe up the spilt tea. It is as if he can't bear to look at her. "But since your infatuation, I'm not allowed near you. You don't want sex with me? You'd rather not sleep in the same bed? Have I got that right?"

"You've got that right." She keeps her voice low and gentle. Julie may seem to be the careless villain of this story, but she has spent years pretending to be someone she is not.

"You bitch," he says. "You bloody fucking bitch!"

"Please don't."

"Please don't what? Be angry, upset?" He shakes his head. "Julie, I could kill you."

She keeps apologising. "I'm so sorry," she says. "I wouldn't hurt you for the world." Even to her ears, the words sound false.

Finally, Mark calms down. He rings his father and explains that Julie is ill. Quietly, they sit together in the front room. Mark puts his head in his hands. Julie makes no move to comfort him. She knows she mustn't give him hope.

After a while, he lifts his head and stares at her. "When did you stop loving me?"

I like you most of the time. You have made me feel confident in myself. I've enjoyed going shopping with you. However pathetic this sounds, it is the truth; but Mark would be horribly hurt, so yet again, she apologises.

*

Julie discovers that she'll miss Mark's mum. Now that she won't be seeing them anymore, she finds she quite likes Mark's siblings, even his dad. These people represent a big chunk of her life. Who will she buy birthday and Christmas cards and presents for now? Who will buy them for her? Donna is the only friend she's ever made. She feels as if she's about to jump into a deep well.

"You'll take the dog with you, of course," Mark says.

Ziggy is on the sofa looking from one beloved face to the other.

Julie is about to assert, "I don't think I can." She loves Ziggy but when she imagines her future, a dog doesn't fit into it. Her eyes fill with tears at the thought of losing Ziggy and then it occurs to her that she must imagine a different future for herself. "Of course, Ziggy comes with me. I love him."

Disgusted – apparently disgusted – Mark turns away. He mumbles something under his breath.

"What did you say?" she asks.

"I said, you're not capable of loving anything."

Taking only a black binbag of clothes and Ziggy, Julie rents a tiny basement flat in a shabby house in North London. There is a garden and nearby Clissold Park to walk her dog. From Habitat she buys pillows and a blue duvet set patterned with snowflakes. Also, a ceramic vase that she places on the cheap melamine coffee table. She lives at the flat for a year, and there is never a day when the vase isn't filled with flowers bought from a market stall. When not at work she spends her time thinking over her life to date while working on two-thousand-piece jigsaw puzzles. She leaves INFO-PULSE and takes a job with a firm of elderly accountants where nobody knows anything about her. At first Julie is fearful; she has never been alone before, but she surprises herself by rarely feeling lonely.

One evening, studying her face in the mirror over the bathroom sink, she decides to cut her shoulder-length hair. She uses kitchen scissors and makes a complete mess of it, but again, when she considers her reflection, she knows that cutting her hair is the right decision.

It's hard to tell which way Julie's thoughts are heading but eventually she goes on her own to the The Duke of Wellington, a lesbian pub she's seen advertised in *Time Out*. The pub is crowded and, standing outside looking in, she almost loses her nerve. *I can always walk straight out again*, she tells herself. At the bar she buys a glass of dry white wine. Almost wistfully she muses on what Mark would think of her now. Glimpsing her reflection in the mirror behind the bar, she realises that she no longer resembles Mark's version of Julie. Her face is tired and her hair looks terrible. She finds an empty table tucked into a corner. Nobody takes any notice of her. She is either invisible or surrounded by a negative force-field declaring Julie Norman to be a lesbian impersonator!

"So, you were a lezzer after all," someone says.

Startled, Julie looks up. "Just a novice," she says, and finds herself smiling.

"Can I join you?" Donna puts her bottle of Budweiser on the table.

"Aren't you with friends?"

"Yes, but I can talk to them any time. I'd rather talk to you."

And they do talk. Both women have changed. Donna is not so carelessly confident whereas Julie – forced to fend for herself – has discovered a measure of confidence. At the end of the evening they go their separate ways.

"Will you be okay?" Donna asks as they stand outside the pub.

"I'll be fine," Julie says. "There's my bus."

As the bus meanders towards Newington Green, Julie wonders why she hadn't brought up Donna's dismissive letter or that disastrous day in Islington. Both marked a turning-point in her life, triggering an unstoppable course of action. But then she remembers her own ambivalence, how appalled she'd been when Alice asked her if she was a lesbian. How ashamed.

Julie joins an art class and a poetry class. She makes a few friends. She still sometimes thinks, *If Mark could see me now*, but really it is better that he doesn't see her because seeing her would only cause him pain. This Julie isn't cute or silly anymore. She doesn't need to be.

Several days later, she bumps into Donna again in Dalston Market, and they go for coffee and this time exchange phone numbers. Neither rings; however, both are now living in North London and sharing several mutual friends, so their paths seem to cross. At a party or in a pub, sometimes Julie will spot Donna's denim-clad shoulders. She'd recognise them anywhere. If Julie stares hard enough, those shoulders will twitch. Donna might shake her head as if trying to dislodge an annoying fly, but eventually, almost with reluctance, she'll turn around and see Julie. A couple of times recently when bumping into Julie like this, Donna has slapped her forehead and exclaimed, "Oh Julie, you pretty thing!"

Julie can't help but be pleased. Yes, she would like to be considered intelligent, thoughtful, a good listener, but nothing quite lifts her heart as much as Donna finding her pretty.

ALPACA MOONLIGHT

"I am not a lesbian," Deirdre sang in a high but surprisingly tuneful voice. "But I'm open to temptation."

"What, you're bi-curious?" I asked.

"Dude, I'd rather eat my own foot than get close up and personal with another woman." She looked thoughtful, then said, "I'm not that keen on getting close up and personal with my Martin either, bless his smelly socks!"

It was a warm afternoon in summer and we were sitting in Deirdre's garden, which is small but raised to give a very distant sea view. (Deirdre insists the sea view adds at least another twenty thousand pounds to the value of her terraced house.) I half-lay, half-lounged on one of her new hardwood recliners, trying to ignore the clank of metal colanders painted in seaside colours that she'd welded into an enormous wind chime and hung from one of the skeletal branches of a dead acer. (I do admire Deirdre's ability to turn her hand to welding, even if she has left large deposits of weld on her fitted carpets that at a glance can easily be mistaken for the misdemeanours of Lord Dudley, her high-maintenance cat.)

"It isn't dead," she insisted – re. the acer, not Lord Dudley. "It's in a state of cryonic hibernation." She followed this statement by rapidly blinking her eyes and instantly I knew that she was quoting something Martin had told her.

I tapped the nearest colander with my index finger, just enough to set the whole edifice moving. A flake of aquamarine paint spiralled down onto the decking. We both stared at it.

With the toe of one faded blue bootee, Deirdre nudged the flake till it disappeared down a crack between the boards, into the hollow area beneath where once the koi carp pond had been.

"I'm off to London tomorrow," I said. "A book launch at Foyles."

"Foyles? Is that like... Bluewater?" She bundled her sheaf of curly hair onto the top of her head and secured it with some garden twine.

"No. It's a big bookshop covering several floors. The author is Elfrida Greenlawne. She's a notable feminist lesbian."

"Never heard of her." Deirdre adopted the sneer in both tone and facial expression she only adopts when talking about poor people, ugly people, smelly people and almost anyone who belongs to or works in a library.

I persevered. "Her writing is a bit like Sarah Waters', only more rural."

"Never heard of *her* either. What about Dan Brown? I've heard of him."

"He's not a feminist lesbian."

"Your point being?" Deirdre said.

We hadn't been getting on since the evening I'd announced that I wanted to be a more visible lesbian and not just *her* best friend. Deirdre had looked up from unwrapping a Cadbury Creme Egg and said, "What's wrong with being my best friend?"

"Nothing at all. But you have Martin and Lord Dudley. It's only natural that I should want a woman to share my life with."

"It doesn't seem natural to me."
"That's because you're straight," I said.
Deirdre answered, "I am what I am," but she looked offended.

Back in Deirdre's garden, she began to spray the foxgloves growing between the paving stones with weed killer.
I said, "Foxgloves are wild flowers, not weeds."
"Well, they're dead wild flowers now. I'll meet you at the bookshop."
"But you don't know where it is."
"Then tell me. It's no big deal, is it?"
And yet it was quite a big deal. Deirdre was perfectly at home in M&S, Debenhams and Evans Outsize. Perfectly at home in Born-to-Dye-Young where she had her blonde highlights enhanced each month, but Deirdre in London, in a bookshop, surrounded by shelves of just... books, that was well outside her comfort zone.

I reached Foyles with at least an hour to spare. Ray's Jazz Cafe was crowded and smelt of wet coats. I settled myself with a coffee and the *Evening Standard* on a stool near the window. Under the guise of puzzling over crossword clues, I glanced around the room, trying to pick out obvious lesbians maybe waiting like myself for the reading, but no, I was the only obvious lesbian.

I'd aimed for a 'womb to womanhood' look. Under normal circumstances I wear a bra, but no bra that evening. 'Let it all hang loose' I'd told myself as I'd towelled dry after a shower, but just in case it was all hanging a little too loosely, I'd added several concealing layers of pea-green: vest, large tee-shirt, followed by gigantic knitted cardigan. My baggy trousers, held up with a leather belt, I hoped combined lesbian chic with artisan credibility. In my pockets I'd stuffed clean handkerchiefs, a tube of peppermints, gum should I need to chew nervously (yet carelessly), big bunch of keys to jingle carelessly (yet quietly) – the keyring bearing an image of a semi-nude Ann Bannon heroine, much loose change and a pearl-handled penknife with several useful attachments that, in my twenty-year ownership, I'd never felt the need to utilise.

Finishing my coffee, I took the stairs up to the third floor. Four rows of chairs were arranged in a semi-circle. On a small table, copies of Elfrida Greenlawne's new novel, *Alpaca Moonlight*, were stacked next to a black and white photograph of the author hugging a sheep.

I sat down in the back row as the all-female audience began to drift in. Hungrily, I watched the women. Here was a club that I didn't yet belong to. Several women browsed the shelves. Why hadn't I browsed the shelves? What could be more natural than a lesbian browsing a shelf of lesbian literature?

An excited murmur ran through the audience as a large woman wearing a flower-patterned kaftan and royal-blue suede bootees, carrying several John Lewis carrier bags, made her way determinedly towards the woman organising the event.

The woman next to me whispered, "That must be Elfrida Greenlawne. She looks nothing like her photograph."

"Actually, that's my friend, Deirdre," I said.

The organiser had made the same mistake. Holding out her hand, she advanced on Deirdre. "Thank you so much for coming all the way from your smallholding in the shadow of the Malvern Hills."

Deirdre ignored her. Like an embattled wild animal, she glared fiercely at the audience.

I stood up and waved, "Deirdre, over here."

She picked up the chair put out for Elfrida Greenlawne and carried it shoulder high to where I was sitting in the back row.

"Budge up so I can get this chair in next to my friend," Deirdre told the woman sitting next to me.

"There's not enough room."

"Of course there is. Just budge up."

Reluctantly, the woman budged up.

Elfrida Greenlawne looked exactly like her photograph, minus the sheep. She wore a large pullover, faded cotton trousers and muddy boots. Her hair was admirably wild, tangled and tawny.

Deirdre hissed, "That woman's not been near a comb in decades."

Thirty minutes later, I was on my feet, clapping and cheering. My mind was full of possibilities that had never occurred to me before. Should I go on a fell-walking holiday? Could I sunbathe topless and swim in icy rock pools? Was it too late to take up kick-boxing, beekeeping, plant husbandry?

I turned to Deirdre to say "Wasn't she great?" but she was already several feet away picking up a book from a display of...

Deirdre flipped the book open in the middle. "Eeugh! Gross! Dude, I'm bringing up my breakfast."

... lesbian erotica.

She tossed it back on the shelf. Head on one side, she began to read out book titles: "*Hot Lesbian Erotica, Best Lesbian Bondage Erotica, Vampire Erotica, Five Minute Erotica* –"

"Deirdre –"

"*The Mammoth Encyclopaedia of Erotica, The Golden Age of Lesbian Erotica* – don't you lesbians have any other interests?"

"It's a display of lesbian erotica."

"It's not for me, dude. I'll meet you in Pizza Hut."

I bought my signed copy of *Alpaca Moonlight* and set off after her. By the time I reached Pizza Hut, she'd already filled her bowl from the salad bar – one for me too, heavy on the croutons, the way Deirdre knows I like.

I sat down.

She speared a tiny tomato and popped it in her mouth before asking, "Do lezzers become lezzers because they're ugly? Or does growing ugly come with the lezzer territory?"

"Excuse me, Deirdre, but lesbians are no uglier than straight people."

"Two Cokes, no ice," Deirdre told the waitress. She turned to me. "I've ordered our pizzas. Fancy swapping half yours for half mine?"

"No," I snapped.

"Oh-oh, there's a lezzer now – it's the woman who didn't want to budge up. Tell me, is there some sort of dress code? Wear anything that nobody in their right mind would want to wear? And by the way, pea green's not your colour – you look as if you're coming down with gastric flu."

"Hello again," the woman said, hesitating at our table. "Elfrida Greenlawne was terrific, wasn't she?"

"She was shite," Deirdre said.

I kicked her under the table.

"A total loser. Smallholding in the shadow of the Malvern Hills... my arse. What she needs," Deirdre stabbed a quarter of hard-boiled egg, "is for some big hairy bloke to give her a good shagging." She looked at me, "And you can stop kicking me under the table because this is a free country and I'm entitled to my opinion."

Two Deirdre-less years passed. I found a girlfriend. We went on a fell-walking holiday and I bathed in an icy rock pool and came down with pleurisy. While I was recovering, my girlfriend met someone else. I joined a kick-boxing class, but may never go topless or keep bees. During all this activity, I didn't once glimpse Deirdre – not even a sighting in Born-to-Dye-Young having her highlights highlighted. And then one morning, just before nine, my bus was stuck in traffic on the high street. I noticed that Marks & Spencer were having a summer sale. Their double doors were still locked but a large blonde-haired woman was ramming the glass with her shoulder. Inside the store, a sales assistant was shaking her head and pointing at her watch.

Deirdre – of course it had to be Deirdre – took a step backwards. I thought she was about to walk away but instead she bellowed, "Dude, will you open this fucking door?"

The following day, I took the train to London. My first stop was Foyles. I climbed the stairs to the second floor and stood in the place I judged Silver Moon Books had once been. It is now called the GLBT section and is full of light, whereas Silver Moon seemed quite dark, which is how I feel a good bookshop should be. I stared down at the woodblock floor and mused that maybe it used to be carpeted and that the carpet once carried an impression of Deirdre's booted feet coming down hard, summoning up every bit of her courage, carrying chair and John Lewis carrier bags towards me through the rows of women so unlike herself. I remembered thinking that she'd looked like an embattled wild animal. Yes, Deirdre was rude, homophobic, could be thoroughly nasty, but what sort of friend had I been? I'd never given a thought to how she was feeling, not just then, but from the moment I'd told her that being *her* best friend just wasn't enough.

Leaving Foyles, I headed for Oxford Street and Deirdre's spiritual home – the bed linen department in John Lewis. I've always been drawn to anything floral and at that moment I felt I desperately I needed a floral hit. And there it was. Perfect. Egyptian cotton, 600 thread, pink tea roses.

In my head I seemed to hear Deirdre's voice. "Step away from that bedding."

My hand reached out to pluck the duvet set from the shelf. "Leave it!"

The voice was at my shoulder. I turned. "Deirdre?"

She held up her hand. "Love means never having to say you're sorry."

"I wasn't intending to say sorry," I replied rather stiffly.

"Me neither."

Deirdre looked different. Her hair was short, her thick golden curls fitting close to her head, which somehow made her face look thoughtful yet animated, rather than tempestuous and over-excitable. Her clothes too were different, less flamboyant; a linen trouser suit, the loose jacket with an unexpected but stylish Nehru collar.

She met my gaze and grinned. "Guess what? I'm a feminist now, as in –" she held her telescopic umbrella in front of her face as if it were a microphone – "*I am strong,*" she sang, "*I am invincible.* Love that word 'invincible'. Who'd have thought someone would stick it in a lyric? Martin says whoever it was should publish a book on how to write a blockbuster hit."

It was as if there'd been no break in our friendship, as if

those times when we'd had nothing kind or nice to say to each other had never been.

I returned the duvet set to the shelf. By unspoken mutual agreement we set off in search of a cafeteria. Standing side by side on the escalator heading upwards, Deirdre said, "I saw you once in that bookshop. You were buying an armload of books. Afterwards I went up to the assistant and said, "I'll take whatever that woman in the pea-green cardigan bought."